When Mike deCosta arrives in Honolulu in search of his missing brother, Luca, his own life is a mess. His ex-boyfriend still has a hold on him, and Luca seems to have made the same mistakes with his abusive ex-lover, Greg. Not only did Luca take Greg back into his life but moved to Honolulu with him in search of Greg's dreams. And now, Luca's been gone for four days and it was the couple's crazy, drug-addled landlady who reported him missing. Not Greg. And now, Greg has vanished, too.

Keanu Māhoe is a private investigator and former cop whose specialty is tracing people who've come from the mainland and slipped through the cracks of Hawaiian society. He's immediately attracted to Mike when they meet on the flight from Los Angeles, and the man's haunting sadness makes Keanu want to reach out and help him. Keanu wants to show Mike the aloha way of life, the value of rainy days and Mondays . . .the other side of paradise.

Rainy Days and Mondays
Copyright © 2020 A.J. Llewellyn
ISBN: 978-1-4874-2857-0
Cover art by Martine Jardin

Published by eXtasy Books Inc or
Devine Destinies, an imprint of eXtasy Books Inc

Look for us online at:
www.eXtasybooks.com or www.devinedestinies.com

Rainy Days and Mondays

By

A.J. Llewellyn

DEDICATION

"Sometimes I'd like to quit
Nothin' ever seems to fit
Hangin' around
Nothin' to do but frown
Rainy days and Mondays
always get me down."

The Carpenters,
Words And music Paul Williams, Roger Nichols

CHAPTER ONE

Mike DeCosta hated Honolulu.

He'd been here forty-five minutes and had never hated a city so damned much in his whole life. The hatred ran deep. He'd hoped never to come back here. And here he was.

Calm down. Deep breath.

Nope. That didn't help. He'd disliked the place the second he set foot off the plane. *Not the first time. But this time. I don't believe in second chances. Not for this island. Never.*

Mike sat behind the wheel of his newly rented lime Jello-green Ford Focus and tried to keep it together. The parking lot of the Jensen rental agency was swamped in darkness, yet still open for business. A new building they said. No outside lights, *yet*.

"But soon!" the woman behind the counter trilled. It didn't help him now, did it?

He stared once more at the gas gauge. Half-empty.

Mike swore, switched off the engine, then got out of the car.

Anxiety bubbled in his chest. Oh, great. It was either that or a heart attack. He needed neither right now. *Calm down. Sheesh.* That would just top off an already horrible day. He stood with his back against the driver side door and took some deep breaths. His panic began to subside, tears in his eyes as he struggled to take in air. Every single calming thought that came to mind seemed to upset him more.

I should have known it was going to be a stinking, lousy day when I woke up and stepped in cat vomit.

He bent over and threw up.

Charming.

He wiped his mouth with the back of his hand, then straightened. He gazed around at the packed lot and eased himself off the car. Even in the darkness, it was obvious the vehicle was dirty. So much for its alleged cleaning.

On shaky legs he walked around it. He wanted to make sure there were no dings on it before he drove it away. In the bad light, he couldn't see any damage to the exterior, but returned to the building to report the half-empty gas tank.

The woman behind the counter was giving grief to some guy about his lack of proof of a return booking code to the mainland.

"I've already explained I'm a local," he said.

"Well, you can't get the discounted rate. Only tourists get that," she snapped.

Geez, she'd been a lot friendlier with Mike, even if she hadn't bothered to come out and check the car over before sending him on his way.

"What do you want?" She swiveled her belligerent attitude over to Mike. Her nametag, partially hidden under a light sweater, revealed her name was Maya. The tag was a little bit off-kilter. Like her personality.

"I've only got a half tank of gas." Mike slid his paperwork toward her. "Can I have it amended on my rental agreement, please?" No sense in paying high island prices for gas to return the car with a full tank. "I checked the car over and didn't notice any damage."

She snatched his papers with an aggrieved air. "All our vehicles are thoroughly inspected and cleaned before they go out again."

Okay, whatever you say, Miss Crankypants.

"We meet again," the man beside him said.

It took Mike a few seconds to realize the guy was talking to him. It was the island man he'd sat next to across the aisle on the flight. That had been a gruesome experience. Narrow rows packed so tightly together and no leg room whatsoever. Every time the guy in front put his seat back he'd hit Mike's face. That's what he got for buying a cheap ticket for an unpleasant education in budget travel—basic economy. It gave him no flexibility beyond boarding the flight. He couldn't upgrade to choose his own seat. He'd been allowed no cabin bag and had been subjected to a severe size restriction on his checked bag. To top it off, he'd been relegated to the last boarding group. Group nine. *Nine!* Mike had never heard of such a thing. There had been only three people in this group and none of them wanted to be in it. Including the guy now smiling at him.

"Oh, yeah, hey," Mike said. He and his neighbor way up in the back seats had swapped greetings and talked a little. They'd even exchanged first names, but Mike couldn't recall the other guy's name now.

"But I already paid for the car," his flight companion told Maya the Merry. "'I only need it for three days.'"

"Oh, okay," she said, as though doing him a huge favor. "Though we don't actually charge your card until you return the vehicle."

Mike already knew this from his own lengthy check-in process.

"Thank you, Maya." Mike picked up his amended paperwork, gave the other guy a wave and took off.

"Aloha," the guy said as Mike left.

Mike nodded, but didn't respond. *Yeah. Aloha. My ass. I wanna go home.*

He gritted his teeth and walked back outside. Unlocking the car door again, he realized he'd left his baggage on the backseat. Anyone could have broken a window and stolen it. He should have put it in the trunk, but the bag was so small, he'd hurled it right where it was.

Once behind the wheel, he focused on breathing deeply

and called Serenity, the woman who owned the bed and breakfast his estranged lover Liam had organized for him. She lived in Hawaii Kai, the neighborhood Luca was living in. He swallowed over the lump in his throat.

God. Luca.

He tried not to fret, but it was hard. Three weeks his brother had been in Honolulu, and three days ago he'd vanished. Luca's lover, Greg, hadn't reported him missing. The woman who'd rented the two men a small room in her house was the one who'd finally called the cops. She, too, lived in Hawaii Kai, and seemed far more concerned than Greg. She had no space for Mike, but after a long argument about his even coming here, Liam had found Mike a room on Craigslist. According to Liam, it was about a mile from Luca and Greg's accommodations.

Mike had tried calling Serenity from the airport but had reached her voicemail. That was another thing. What the hell kind of name was Serenity? He left a second message for the woman. She knew he was coming tonight. He checked the time. Eight P.M. and the island city seemed shrouded in darkness. He had no idea how to get to her, and since he'd opted not to get GPS for the car, he was completely clueless. He could use his cell phone navigation but it would chew up his data. He'd allowed Liam to talk him into downgrading his cell phone plan to save money.

He had me nickel and diming myself while he was busy splurging on our joint funds! Once again, Mike mentally jotted the cost of the GPS. He had no idea how long he'd be here, and Liam would go berserk at the idea that he was spending more money, but he had no choice. He was here to find his brother. He couldn't deal with driving around a city he didn't know anymore.

And hated.

Mike got out once again and approached the rickety wooden stairs to the building.

Maya's going to think I've got a crush on her or something . . .

When the Honolulu Police Department had called Mike that morning with the news, he'd been devastated. He'd never liked Greg and had worried when Luca had reunited with his on-again, off-again lover. When Luca had told him he and Greg were moving to Honolulu, a lifelong dream for both of them, Mike had begged him not to rush into things.

And now Luca was gone.

He just keeps picking the wrong guys. What if Greg did something to him?

His cell phone rang. *Liam.* Mike took the call, unable to keep the anguish from his voice.

"Have you heard anything? Has he tried to call?"

Mike had transferred his landline calls to his cell phone, but occasionally, Luca had been known to reach out to Liam when he didn't wish to be interrogated by Mike.

"Nope. Nothing. You got there in one piece, I take it?"

Mike winced at the chill in his ex's voice. Liam would be pissed for weeks that he'd come out here, but how could he not? Luciano, or Luca to everyone who knew him, was his only family. Neither man spoke to their parents who lived in Corpus Christi, Texas. The two brothers were very close.

A long pause. Things hadn't been good between him and Liam for a long time. Now it was beyond rocky. A pharmacist by trade, Mike had given it up to open a health café with Liam.

It had been a total disaster. Shuttered after only six months, Mike had been forced to return to working late hours at various drugstores. He'd just scored a fulltime gig when he got the news about his brother. His new employer had given him an ultimatum. Mike had chosen his brother.

It hurt to know he'd be back to job hunting once he returned to LA, but the truth was, his brother was more important than any job.

And next to his brother, writing mystery novels was the

other most cherished aspect of his life. He had landed his first book contract and was in the middle of his third round of edits. Lord, if he'd known how complex the whole publishing industry was, he might have stuck to the pharmaceutical industry.

He thought again. No. He could handle edits. His editor was awesome and so supportive. She often put smiley faces next to his best lines. He lived to make her laugh. Maybe his luck would change now that he'd decided he and Liam were really over, and to focus on his writing.

"Are you there?" Liam asked, his tone icier than ever.

"I'm here."

"What's the house like?"

"No idea. I can't contact her. I've left her two messages."

A sharp intake of breath. "Can't you just drive there?"

"I don't have the address. I know it's Hawaii Kai. I don't even know how to get there."

"Wait. She got back to me and I made a note of the address. I texted it to you. You didn't get it?"

"Not yet." Mike checked his cell phone. He could hear Liam tapping into his computer. "Nope. No text." He inhaled deeply. "I'm going to get a GPS. I'll need it anyway since I've got to meet with the police." He glanced beside him at the piece of notepaper with the scrawled directions for the police station for District Seven, covering the eastern city neighborhoods, including Hawaii Kai. He was due to call a Detective Ng at nine o'clock in the morning.

When last he'd spoken to the detective heading the investigation, he'd said they had no leads on his brother and no way to search for him without information from Greg.

Detective Ng had asked Mike to meet with Greg before they talked.

"This guy is being really unhelpful," the detective had said on the phone. "Maybe he'll open up to you more."

Mike doubted it.

"Okay, here's the address," Liam said. "It's one seven one seven Kumukumu Street. Right off the main road, Lunalilo Home Road." He stumbled over the unfamiliar words. "It's about three miles up toward the mountain." He gave him the zip code and said, "I guess you should get the GPS, now that you're there, but you're not a private detective, Mike. You should leave this in the hands of the police."

Fuck you, Liam. Mike sat rigid in the car. "If you went missing I'd come looking for you," he said.

"*I* wouldn't go missing. I'm not a dumbass like your brother."

"*Anyone* can go missing." Mike fought to keep his temper in check. It had been like this for weeks between them. This conversation tipped him over the edge, though. When he went home he'd make sure Liam took out every last item of clothing he'd 'forgotten' to take with him. And the rest of his goofy DVDs. The guy had a passion for beetle fighting and tree shaping. Who knew there were so many DVDs about both?

Constantly needing to pick up needed items had been a pathetic ruse, but Mike tried to avoid conflict with his former lover as much as possible. Liam had moved out six weeks ago, but for Mike, it had been over for three months, ever since he'd discovered Liam had been embezzling from their joint company funds.

Liam still didn't know that Mike was aware of what had been going on. But he soon would. *Maybe this is a blessing in disguise that I won't be there when he's arrested. God. What the hell was he thinking borrowing all that money from the Small Business Association?*

Luca's disappearance was the capper to an unpleasant time for them. They'd agreed to separate, but they both owned the house in West Hollywood. Liam had moved out only when things became impossible. Now the place was on the market and Liam had the keys. He was supposed to feed the cat and meet any realtors who wanted to show the place.

As long as he doesn't try moving back in, we'll be fine.

"I think I should move *all* my things out when you get back," Liam said, as though reading his thoughts.

"Okay, no problem." A violent headache began behind Mike's eyes. *A migraine. Man, can I take any more stress today?* "If that's your decision." He wanted Liam to feel he had the upper hand. He was certain his ex would change his mind, but right now he didn't care. It was a relief to know that it was finally over. No more dopey reasons to stop by.

"I'm sure I left my first edition copy of M.L. Rhodes' *The Draegan Lords* here . . ." That was a typical lie. Liam couldn't *live* without the author's books. He just wanted an excuse to snoop and check for evidence of another man. The only man in Mike's life had hair. A lot of it. He'd ask his friend Heidi to take Herman home for a few days. She'd been the one to help save Herman from the mean streets of downtown L.A. after all.

Now Mike said nothing. He'd given Liam the upper hand, which Liam would enjoy more than a thirty-percent discount coupon for Macy's.

Mike was the one who'd said, "Let's do it or let's not do it. Not both." He couldn't deal with the emotional fallout right now. There was too much to do.

I can accept that it's over. Let him take everything. Except the cat. Having Liam out of there is a load off my mind. No wonder I have a headache. Food. I need to eat. I haven't eaten all day.

"That's my decision," Liam said, his stone huffy.

"Well, okay, then." Mike squeezed the bridge of his nose with thumb and forefinger. His head pounded relentlessly.

Liam hung up on him. It sucked to think Mike was in this alone. He had allowed Liam to isolate him from all his friends, and rectifying that had caused ruptures in his relationship with Liam. But even now, reconnecting with his closest friends remained in a fragile state. There was nobody to call. Mike could call Heidi about Herman. Animals were her only thing in life. She could handle taking care of the little guy. Maybe she was right not to trust people.

Mike put his head against the cool window. In a crisis he'd usually call Luca, but now Luca *was* the crisis.

I have to see my brother again.

He got out once again and returned to the car rental agency. His flight companion was immobile, waiting, slumped against the counter.

"You still here?" Mike asked, surprised.

"Yeah. You can't stay away either, huh?"

Mike gave the desk clerk a sheepish look. "I need to get a GPS. When you're ready." He indicated to the man beside him.

Maya arched a brow at Mike. She'd suggested the GPS in the first place but he'd declined.

She found him one and charged it to his card. This time she opted to come outside with him and show him how to set it up. Mike suspected she was enjoying making the other guy wait. She shot him a smug a look over her shoulder. "I won't be long."

He shook his head but said nothing, reaching into his pocket for his cell phone.

Outside, Maya marched toward Mike's car. "We won't take a final tally for the GPS. We'll add it to your bill when you return it."

Of course you will.

At the vehicle, she took the keys from him, let herself inside, then switched on the interior light. She unpacked the GPS system from its box.

"I'll put the instructions in the glove compartment." She leaned across, popped it open and a ton of papers fell out of it.

"Unlock the passenger door. I'll pick them up," he said.

Maya pressed the button for the universal lock. He climbed in beside her, trying to follow her rapid instructions as he gathered the papers that clearly belonged to the previous renter.

"This is *your* rental agreement," she said, when he handed her the pile.

"No, mine's on the dashboard." He pointed to it.

"De Costa," she enunciated as though he were very stupid. She pointed at it with an artificial fingernail painted to look like leopard spots. He could imagine her clawing him within an inch of his life.

He stared at the name. No. It couldn't be. *Luciano De Costa.* He scanned the rest of the document. His brother had rented this very same vehicle five days ago. Mike almost wept when he saw Luca's scrawled signature. He had used his California driver's license to secure the same eight-dollar-a-day deal Mike had.

I had no idea he even used this rental car company.

"This isn't mine," he said. "I can't believe it. My brother rented this car."

Maya scrunched up her nose. "Really?" She grabbed the page from him. "Oh, God. This is the guy who never brought the damned car back." She swiveled her gaze in Mike's direction, a look of concern on her face. "We had to get this towed off the Old Pali Road when he wouldn't return our calls."

"When did you get the car back?"

"This afternoon." She gave him a fish-eyed look. "I hope you're going to be more reliable."

She couldn't have known his brother had disappeared, so he let the comment slide.

"Guess the guys didn't have time to clean the car properly." She reached out to brush some dust off the dash.

"Don't!" he yelled, making her jump. "Don't touch anything else!"

He stretched his arm across her, as she stared at him, a

stricken expression on her face. "What? What is it?"

His cell phone rang. He checked the readout. Liam again. He debated taking the call. He didn't want to talk to him, but what if Luca had called him in distress?

Mike took the call.

"I'm sorry." Liam sounded upset. "I know I'm being an ass."

"I can't talk right now." Mike glanced at the woman beside him. "I've just found the rental car my brother apparently drove."

"Where?" Liam asked.

"Gotta go. I'll get back to you. I have to report this to the cops." He glanced at Maya beside him. "We both need to get out very slowly and not touch another thing."

"Why?"

"We can't disturb any more evidence."

"Evidence!"

He closed his eyes for a second. *I hope his body isn't in the trunk.*

Mike ended the call with Liam and dialed 911.

CHAPTER TWO

The 911 operator was not very helpful. Not much *aloha* in her attitude, until he told her his brother was missing and the police had called him in Los Angeles that morning.

"I just arrived on the island and rented a car. I found some papers belonging to the person who had it before me. I know it sounds crazy, but it was my brother. He took out the same vehicle five days ago. The Jensen lady told me he failed to return it—"

"The Jensen lady?"

"Yes. Jensen. It's a car rental company. A new one."

"Never heard of it."

"Like I said, it's new. I'm in the parking lot. Can the police come out here?"

"Okay," the operator said. "Are you still in the car?"

"No. We got out."

"Do I have to be a part of this?" Maya whined.

"Yes," the operator, who'd clearly heard her, said in unison with Mike.

"I'm in space number thirty," Mike told the operator. Of course, his other line rang. His briefly illuminated iPhone screen showed him it was Serenity, his Happy Hippie Hawaiian landlady. He'd have to call her back.

"What's the address?" the operator asked.

Mike rattled off the first part of the Nimitz Highway location Maya gave him.

"Holy cow!" Maya suddenly shouted. "I left the other customer inside." She picked up her long, trailing skirt and

12

bolted for the building, leaving Mike to deal with giving the operator the rest of the address. He had no clue what it was and nothing appeared on the paperwork he examined by leaning into the car to check under the light the clerk had left on.

The operator interrupted him. "I have it. I'll have a unit right out to you, Mr. DeCosta."

She must have sent out a crew working the airport, unless the island was really that small and a cop was just a stone's throw away.

Two uniformed officers rolled in, their vehicle stopping a few feet from him. They stepped outside. He noticed they weren't as cute as the extras that played beat cops on *Hawaii Five-O*, but he greeted them with relief.

Once again, he repeated his story. As he spoke, the man from the plane who'd been stuck in the Jensen office all this time, came out, turning his head toward Mike. He seemed to hesitate, then kept moving.

"I've been in touch with Detective Ng at your Diamond Head precinct," Mike told the uniformed officers.

Neither cop registered recognition of the detective's name. One of them said, "Oh, that's East Honolulu, District Seven. You say he called you this morning?"

"Yes. I live in Los Angeles and Detective Ng contacted me and told me that my brother Luca has been missing for three days. His lover never reported this to the police, but the landlady they're renting from did."

"And you hopped on a plane and came out here?" The second officer asked.

"Yes."

"Have you spoken to the lover?"

Mike shook his head. "I was going to. I didn't want to call until I got here because I figured I'd be harder to blow off if I was here. I wanted to talk to him tonight. Detective Ng asked me to wait and speak to him in person. It's a crazy coincidence I know, but I just rented this car and the desk clerk and I found a bunch of papers in the glove compartment. It looks like my brother rented this car but never returned it. She said they had to trace it and tow it back from the old . . ." He frowned trying to remember the name of the road. "I think she said something about an old pali."

The first officer nodded. "The Old Pali Road. Hmm." He exchanged a weighted glance with the other cop. Mike caught it from the interior light of the vehicle.

"What?" Mike asked.

The cops exchanged another significant look before the first one said, "Well, it's kind of remote up there. Lots of trails. Maybe he fell off the Pali, or got injured. Or . . ."

They all looked at each other.

Mike swallowed over the hard lump in his throat. *Or, somebody pushed him. What if he is alive and calling for help? What if he's . . . dead?*

I just know something really bad happened to Luca.

The officers were very calm and methodical. They called Detective Ng at the number Mike gave them. He instructed them to check the trunk and said he wanted the vehicle towed to the Diamond Head police headquarters for further processing.

Mike shivered, although it wasn't cold, as the officers donned gloves. Using flashlights, they searched the vehicle.

A crime scene technician arrived and took Mike's fingerprints and Maya's. The desk clerk seemed very unhappy about this turn of events.

"You need lights in this parking lot," one of the officers told her.

"I know. New building." She must have been so sick of saying that. She corroborated everything Mike had told them. Both Maya and Mike held their breaths as one of the officers unlocked the trunk.

Nothing.

"I need to talk to the person who picked up the car," the first officer told Maya.

"It took us two days to track it down," she griped. "GPS isn't exactly quick on locating things on the island. Anyway, this afternoon two of our guys went up to the Pali, but I think it was Eddie who actually drove it back here."

"Is Eddie here now?"

"No, but I can call him if you need to talk to him."

"Yes. Please call him immediately. Has anyone else touched the vehicle since it came back?" Before she could respond, he turned to Mike. "We got a stroke of luck that the car wasn't washed before you picked it up."

"You're right." Mike nodded. *And to think I was pissed at first.*

"We'll need to talk to your brother's boyfriend," the officer told him. "What's his number?"

Mike gave it to them, but Greg's cell phone was turned off and the call went straight to voicemail. Mike also provided the address and phone number where Greg and Luca had been staying. They got the landlady's voicemail, too.

As the three men spoke, Mike became aware of somebody watching them. It was the guy from the plane. He sat behind the wheel of a snazzy sports car, top down.

"Is everything okay?" he asked. He fixed Mike with a hard stare.

Mike's shoulders sagged. No. Everything was not okay. He tried hard to act as though he stood around parking lots with police officers all the time. His silence must have spoken volumes because the guy stepped out of the vehicle.

"Are you all right?" He walked up to Mike and squeezed his shoulder.

"I came here to find my missing brother. By some strange coincidence, he rented this very same car. Jensen had to tow it back from The Old Pali Road this afternoon. My brother never returned it."

Even in the darkness, Mike could see the sympathy in the other man's eyes.

"Oh, wow. I'm so sorry. I wondered why you seemed so stressed out on the plane." He glanced around at the cops. "I'm a private investigator. If I can help in any way, please contact me. He flipped a card from his pocket and handed it to Mike.

"You stinkin' up the joint, Keanu?" one of the cops asked, making his way over to the private eye.

"Hey, Noah." Keanu unleashed a toothy smile and they shook hands.

Noah was the first cop Mike had spoken to, and he now wondered how the hell he hadn't remembered Keanu's name when they'd spoken on the flight. Keanu wasn't exactly a common name to him and there was the movie star with the same name.

Now that he looked at him, Keanu was a very handsome man, in a long, dark-haired kind of way. He was tall and solid. He didn't look Hawaiian, but then Mike didn't really know what a Hawaiian man looked like anymore. Keanu was a cool mix of ethnicities as far as he could tell.

It didn't take long for the officers to turn their attention away from the shaggy P.I. He took the hint, turned to Mike and said, "I'll be on my way. If you need anything, let me know."

"Thanks."

As soon as Keanu had driven away, the second officer approached Mike. "Do you know if your brother's boyfriend drove this vehicle?"

"I didn't even know my brother drove it until I was inside it."

"Oh, right. Of course. You had any luck contacting Greg? What's his last name?"

"Prentiss." Mike couldn't help the venom dripping from his voice. "And no. I've had no luck."

"We'll take a drive out there," Noah said. "Come with us and we'll bring you back to rent another vehicle." He gestured toward Mike's car. "We're towing it away for processing."

Mike nodded. Maya came out with a fresh set of paperwork and key for him.

"Your new vehicle is in slip seventy-two. We're open until eleven P.M." She turned to the officers. "I've tried calling Eddie and Mano, the two guys who went to pick up the car. I can't reach either of them. Here are their numbers." She handed Noah a piece of paper.

A tow truck pulled into the lot and, after an exchange of greetings, the driver loaded up the car.

Mike gripped his small suitcase, wondering yet again where the hell his brother was and if he was okay.

He got into the police vehicle after stowing his things in the trunk. Noah had the wheel, his partner, Alvin, was talking about chicken teriyaki, and Mike sat in back, suddenly starved once more, listening to the endless litany of car thefts and vandalism reports on the radio.

"Lots of burglaries," he commented.

"Yeah, we get a ton of those." Noah caught Mike's gaze in the rearview mirror when they stopped at a light. "We get more of those than anything else. Missing persons cases are rare."

"Really?" Mike was curious. The way the two officers exchanged looks told him Noah wasn't being truthful.

"People come here to kinda disappear off the grid," Noah said, finally.

"That doesn't sound like my brother." *I hope.* "When you do get missing person cases, do they usually involve locals or tourists?"

"Both."

"Usually tourists," Alvin interjected. "They love going for hikes to places they've found online and have no clue about." There was bitterness in his tone.

Mike winced. "What is the Old Pali Road?"

The two officers turned their heads toward one another again. Finally Noah spoke.

"It's a very old mountain road. It has a lot of secret trails leading off it."

Mike closed his eyes and leaned his head back against the seat. He was in agony now, pain throbbing behind his left eye. He wanted to study the view but felt really bad now.

"You okay?" Noah asked.

"Bad migraine."

"My wife gets those. You need to stop and pick up something?"

"Is that okay?"

"No problem."

Noah made a turn and pulled over a few minutes later outside a 7-Eleven on Dillingham Boulevard. Man, he could have been back in Los Angeles, the way these stores all looked the same. Mike thanked the officer and went inside. He picked up a bottle of Excedrin, the only thing that worked on his headaches, an ice-cold bottle of soda and an apple. He wasn't sure about the array of greasy-looking pastries.

Back inside the vehicle, he took two pills, washing them down with soda. He took a couple of bites of apple. They stuck in his throat. He felt just like Snow White.

Noah took nondescript surface streets until they saw a sign saying *Waikiki* and Mike felt a small thrill. He just wished he'd come here under different circumstances.

To his right, waves rolled along the shoreline. He didn't recognize anything, but then again, it had been a long time since his last trip. Alvin veered away from the coast and moved up toward a mountain road.

They hit the freeway and Mike struggled to take it all in.

Traffic was unbelievable. He hadn't expected that. In truth, he'd expected open roads. In his fantasies, he'd envisioned hula girls with baskets of coconuts on their heads and maybe some horses and buggies. He'd seen enough movies and TV shows to know that Hawaii was more cosmopolitan than that, but it really shocked him to find he was knee-deep in an endless traffic jam. He couldn't recall much from his first—and last time—here. But he'd been seven and Luca had been five. He took a deep breath and swigged at the soda again.

Noah took the shoulder of the freeway to bypass the worst snarls and, after spotting palm trees and a cluster of shiny high rises to his right, a sign said Freeway End. They picked up speed as they emptied out with dozens of other vehicles onto clogged surface streets in varying stages of construction.

They kept going until they hit the ocean. It did look beautiful in the dark. Palm trees swayed and people walked their dogs along the breakfront. A sign read Kalanianaole Highway. They turned left.

Mike struggled to pronounce the name in his mind and gave up.

"Not long now," Noah said. They made another left after several long, congested blocks onto Halemaumau Street. *Man, I'll never be able to pronounce these Hawaiian names.*

At a flat, dun-colored building out of which throbbed techno music that wasn't his brother's taste at all, the police vehicle stopped. All three occupants looked at the house.

"They're a bit loud," Noah said and opened his door.

Mike and Alvin joined him on the sidewalk, and under actual streetlights and through filmy curtains in the front room, Mike detected shadowy figures moving inside the house. It was weird, as though people were drifting at slow speed. It was even stranger considering the frenetic beat of the music.

Mike had an odd flashback to an old episode of *Dragnet*,

where Sgt. Joe Friday takes on a young junkie whose face was half-painted in blue. He was known as Blue Boy.

"Ice," Noah said, with a grimace. Mike's uneasiness began to grow. He'd seen enough old episodes of *Dog, the Bounty Hunter* to know that ice was the apparent scourge of the islands.

"No ice in paradise," was Dog's mantra, but it looked to be a losing battle. Methamphetamine was a rampant mainland problem and it had spread like the disease that it was, to the island state. Mike knew all too well. He was a pharmacist trained to look for signs of customers buying weird chemicals in bulk.

"I'm calling in for backup." Alvin shot Mike a glance. "They won't be long. I know you're anxious, but we don't know what we're walking into."

"No problem. I appreciate your help." Mike stared at the figures inside the house again. A woman was dancing in a bizarre way, arms stretched above her head.

He thought about the *Dragnet* episode again and how Blue Boy kept telling people he wanted to go 'far out, man,' and he did, all the way to a death by overdose. Mike yearned to run to the house and break down the front door. What if his brother was in there somewhere? Dead?

It took several minutes for the second unit to arrive, and Mike ignored all requests to remain outside and followed the officers to the house. Noah knocked on the door and it took several more minutes for somebody to answer it.

The young man who greeted them peered out of the semi-darkness, eyes pinned like a cat's. *Hoo-boy*. He was flying high on something.

"Can I help you?" A flicker of alarm registered in his crazy eyes.

"Turn the music down," Alvin shouted.

"What?"

Noah repeated the request.

"Oh." The young man turned and retreated into the house.

The officers and Mike pounced on the open entryway, swarming the front room. The music still boomed, hitting Mike right in the solar plexus, making him feel nauseous. What he saw when the music suddenly stopped and lights came on, shocked him to the core.

He'd never seen anything like this.

There were weeping girls sprawled on stained mattresses on the floor in the hallway. A weird odor permeated the residence. The metallic tang hit the back of Mike's throat and he recognized it immediately. They were cooking meth here. There was a reason the drug was so popular. It was easy to produce using household chemicals, but those same products went into addicts' bodies. He'd seen firsthand the destruction and agony it caused.

Everywhere he looked, people seemed to be lying or throwing up on mattresses lined up and leaving no space empty.

"Christ on a rock," one of the cops said. "I've heard about these places but I've never seen one here in Hawaii Kai before."

The police called for ambulances. The stench of human waste and vomit was stifling. Mike spotted a kitty litter box and wondered where its occupant was. From what he could tell, whoever owned or had the lease on the house had rented out every last inch of floor space.

Greg was nowhere to be found. As Mike and the officers systematically went through the rooms, more and more mattresses were discovered. In one bedroom, the landlady lay on her bed, smoking a joint, her cat sitting Sphinx-like on her chest. The woman looked surprised to see the police busting into her room. Alvin and Noah, in turn, looked equally stunned that her room seemed calm and orderly in the face of the chaos beyond its closed door.

Kelly Park would have been an attractive Asian woman of indeterminate age, if she hadn't been renting a house of horrors. Her red satin kimono slipped as she jumped in fright. The expanse of boobage she flashed was more than Mike ever wanted to see.

She removed headphones from her ears and sat up on the bed, the cat sulkily crawling away from her. "What's up?" she asked, flicking gazes at them all. "If you're here about the music, I told them to keep it down. Useless users." She flicked a gaze at Mike. "Who the hell are you?"

Before he could respond, Noah introduced them.

"Oh, yes. Luca's brother. He talks about you. Said something about how you're a pharmacist and some kind of mystery novelist. Here's a mystery for you, where is he now?"

Mike just stared at her. She was weird. *Really* weird. He recalled now that one of Luca's earliest emails said as much. *Weird, but kind. I think those were his words. I need to check.*

She got off the bed, leaving the cat to curl up with a resentful air on her pillow. Kelly didn't seem to take too kindly to the police firing off intrusive questions about why she was running a drug house.

"It didn't start that way." Her tone turned whiny. "I came from the mainland three years ago and I was forced to start renting out rooms about a year ago. One thing led to another. Tenants would bring friends, and everyone was willing to pay the same rent, even for a mattress. I lost my job at Hilo Hattie's." She flickered a glance at Mike. "It used to be the hottest chain of stores in the islands. There's only one left in Honolulu now."

She appeared hazy and out of it, her gaze falling to the floor. He glanced down, noticing her bruised feet. He wondered if they were the result of medication. He'd seen this pattern before. He swallowed. Hard. Petechiae and purpura on the legs, probably due to medication-induced vasculitis.

Mike eyed the vials beside her bed. "Are you taking medication for typhus?" he asked.

She gaped at him. "You're good. Your brother told me you'd know what caused these bruises."

Mike stared at her feet. "You must be in a lot of pain."

"Hell yah, sunshine. That's why I smoke weed and lie up in bed all day."

"Typhus?" Noah looked uneasy. "Isn't that contagious?"

"No. I don't think she has Typhus. Probably did, at one point, right?" Mike held Kelly's gaze.

She fidgeted, looked uncomfortable and averted her gaze. "Yeah," she mumbled.

"Typhus is a bacterium, but it looks like she's on strong antibiotics and her skin is no longer yellow." Mike glanced at the vials again. "I can't believe a reputable doctor would have prescribed so many courses of such a heavy antibiotic."

Her cheeks flamed.

"How did you get Typhus?" Mike worked hard to keep his tone gentle. If he could get enough information from her, the cops around them could use it to bust what was beginning to look like a phony prescription scam.

When she said nothing, he repeated the question.

"Head lice," she said. "One crawled into my ear. I was in agony for two weeks."

The cops groaned and edged away from her.

"So they gave you pain meds to go along with the antibiotics. And even though the infection is gone, you've developed a secondary illness, which is much worse than the original disease," Mike said. "You're taking the antibiotics so you can get the pain meds." He picked up a bottle and groaned.

OxyContin, otherwise known as hillbilly heroin.

Mike grabbed Noah's arm. "We need to get her to a hospital. Those bruises are an indication that her veins are seizing up."

"We can't do that. She's under arrest." Noah sounded aghast.

"Arrest? I can't be arrested!" The landlady looked horrified. "I'm teaching hula classes in the morning! They've all pre-paid."

"Lady, you won't last the night if you don't get help. Now." Mike wished he hadn't glimpsed the woman's feet. He wished he could focus on his brother, and not her litany of self-pitying excuses. He wanted to harden his heart to her plight.

"I'll call for an ambulance," Alvin said, sounding aggrieved. He stepped out of the room. As Noah began peppering Kelly with questions again, Mike said, "You'd better lie down, feet higher than your heart." He arranged pillows beneath her knees.

"Oh, I can breathe again." She closed her eyes. Her skin was a terrible color. He was afraid she'd passed out, but she finally spoke, her voice weak.

"I'm working two jobs and renting out this place. Some of the tenants have been here for months. Mostly the people bring their friends, all word of mouth. I haven't had to advertise for a long time." She glanced up Mike, her eyes feverish. "Greg is my sister's son. That's why I felt a responsibility to Luca."

"Where is Greg now?" Mike asked. Once she was taken away, he'd never get to ask her questions.

"No idea. He took off right after I called the police. Somebody slashed my tires. Can you beat that? I'm assuming it was him, out of retaliation."

"Are Greg and my brother using drugs?" Mike braced himself for the answer.

"Only mild stuff. A bit of weed."

"You're in a lot of trouble," Noah told her, "Running a drug den."

"I'm not running a drug den!" she shouted, half rising from the pillows. "I rent space to needy tourists. It's not my problem if they're all addicts!"

Mike ran a hand across his face. His headache was getting worse and he knew he was going to barf.

"I'm gonna throw up," he announced.

The landlady's eyes widened and she pointed to a door to his left. The smell inside the bathroom was awful. Sickly sweet strawberry incense and . . . cat waste. Neither stench helped. He was sick in the grimy toilet bowl.

When he washed his face afterward, he stared at his expression in the bathroom mirror. His skin was mottled, his eyes flushed.

I want to go home and sleep for a hundred years.

Back in her room, Kelly pointed to a backpack in the corner. "It belongs to your brother. I found it tucked up on his mattress a few days ago. He'd tried to make it look like he was sleeping. He'd bunched up some of his clothes with it, but everything else he brought here is gone, by the way. When I first went into the room, I thought he might have OD'd or something so I tried to wake him up." Her voice trailed away as he took the backpack from her.

Luca never went anywhere without it. Mike thought he might barf again, not that he had anything left in him. He glanced at Noah, who nodded.

"Open it, Mike. Maybe there's a note or something in it." He turned an accusatory glance at the landlady. "I thought you said Greg and Luca aren't drug users."

She threw up her hands. "They're not. But they're adventure seekers. They climbed the Stairway to Heaven last week and got ticketed by a cop."

"Stairway to Heaven?" Mike asked, as he unzipped the backpack. He steeled himself for whatever he might find. Back in LA, Luca always carried notebooks, pens, his wallet and iPad, as well as numerous gadgets to keep the portable electronic notebook functioning.

"It's a very dangerous trail nobody is supposed to use," Alvin said, his tone terse. "Not even locals." He stopped talking. There was complete silence as Mike revealed a plastic bag filled with stones.

It was the first time he'd experienced anything close to relief and actual breathing since the painful call from Detective Ng that morning.

"Did you put these in here?" Noah asked the landlady.

"Of course not. I looked inside when he disappeared. When I saw the stones, I had an idea he might be okay, that he might have taken off to get away from Greg. He seemed so unhappy with him, but he promised me if he ever did leave, he'd let me know. I haven't heard from him in a couple of days and got really worried. Of all my tenants, he's a love bug."

"Thank you," Mike told her, holding her gaze. He owed her that much. Without her intervention, drug den or not, had she not contacted the police, his brother's disappearance would still be a secret.

The outer pockets of the backpack were empty. It seemed as though Luca had planned to be gone for some time – or that he didn't intend to return at all.

But why didn't he call me and tell me?

Because he didn't want me to judge him. Maybe he just wanted time to think. But what about the abandoned car?

Mike shouldered his brother's backpack, his thoughts going in circles. Suddenly, the sound of wailing sirens pierced the night.

"Show us where they've been sleeping," Alvin said, his tone urgent.

Kelly didn't look happy as she led Mike and the officers toward the garage, where Greg and Luca had been sleeping. She appeared to be unsteady on her feet. "They paid extra to sleep out there." She handed Alvin a key to the padlocked door. "I don't feel so good," she mumbled.

The first paramedics arrived and she stumbled into their arms, right there on the path between her house and the garage.

They loaded her onto a gurney. Mike would have explained his findings to the paramedics, but the cops had taken over the scene. One of them handed over her bagged medication bottles to a paramedic, who read the labels, squinting in the bad light.

Another paramedic placed an oxygen mask over her face. She relaxed and looked like she'd gone off to dreamland.

Glad she can sleep. Mike wished he could burrow under some covers himself. He couldn't wait for this day to end.

He followed Alvin and Noah into the garage where they found it a lot neater and cleaner than the main house. A double mattress lay atop some bedsprings. Somebody had made the bed in haste. The rest of the place was orderly, some men's clothing hanging in a weathered wooden closet.

He sniffed. God. It was the dreadful, cheap cologne Greg always wore. It lingered on the air wherever the man went. Mike wondered, not for the first time, how his brother tolerated the stench.

Screams filled the air, and the three men all rushed out of the converted garage.

Police and paramedics were escorting the stoned tenants from the main house into ambulances out front. One young man had become so combative, he was put into a straight-jacket. He hollered like crazy, his hair standing on points, his glasses askew on his face.

"Help me!" he shrieked, looking Mike right in the eye.

Of course, there was nothing Mike could do. The poor man's wretched state rattled him to the core. The man was in a bad mental state. Back home in LA, Mike and Liam had once

come across a teenage couple on a hike on the Holy Jim mountain trail of the Cleveland National Forest. The woman had
run to Mike, screaming about a python trying to eat her. Neither he nor Liam could find a python anywhere.

When her partner said tigers had been stalking them, Mike
suspected they'd come up to the trail to smoke methamphetamine. He'd called 911 from his cell phone when the young
man claimed Jesus was following him and that worms were
eating his brains.

The girl sipped imaginary water from a straw that was actually a tree branch.

Man, those drugs are a real menace to society.

Just like that pair, Mike had to let the professionals take
care of the guy trussed up in the straightjacket.

"We'll take you back to the car rental agency," Alvin told
Mike. "We can't do much more tonight. We can't organize a
manhunt. It's too dark up on the Pali. Detective Ng will contact you in the morning about your brother's cell phone records and any other questions he might have."

As he was about to get in the car with the officers, another
vehicle pulled up behind them. It was Keanu. He got out of
his convertible and walked toward Mike, the look on his face
intense.

"Maya, the friendliest car rental agent alive gave me this
address. I thought I'd swing by and see if I could help."

"Yeah, you can," Alvin said. "You can take him to pick up
his car. We just got a call for a domestic disturbance up the
hill from here."

"It would be my pleasure." Keanu gave him the kind of
look Mike thought only happened in movies. He couldn't remember the last time he'd felt a genuine frisson of pleasure
shooting up his spine this way. He could get used to it. He
could get used to it *a lot*.

Mike took possession once again of his belongings,

transferring them and Luca's backpack to the trunk of Keanu's rented sports car. He bid farewell to the police and got into the passenger seat beside Keanu.

They pulled away from the curb right behind the police car, and in front of that, an ambulance drove, its interior lights blazing.

Mike gave an involuntary shiver as he stared at the face of the man in the straightjacket, sitting up, staring out at Mike. His glasses were still crooked and his face had taken on a fierce scowl.

"Who the hell's he?" Keanu asked. "And what was with all the ambulances?"

Mike sighed. "Long story." He put his forehead to the cool window glass. He took a couple of deep breaths.

"It's going to be okay," Keanu said.

For some strange reason, Mike believed him.

CHAPTER THREE

Mike tried calling his landlady, Serenity, as they headed back to the highway. Once again he got her voicemail, and he ended the call. He checked his voicemail, remembering that she'd called earlier. She'd left a message apologizing for being unavailable until eleven o'clock that night.

"I'm having dinner at the airport with my daughter," Serenity said. "She's leaving the island tonight, going back to school on the mainland. My place is kinda complicated to find. As soon as I'm close to Hawaii Kai, I'll call. We can arrange to meet on Lunalilo Home Road, and you can follow me up the mountain."

"Eleven o'clock?" Keanu shook his head when Mike repeated all of this to him. "That's not very convenient of her, but it is for us."

"It is?" Mike was worried now. Serenity had rambled a bit in her message and had said that she preferred not to leave a key under her mat for him, even if Mike did have a GPS system and could find his own way to her.

"My place is quiet, and the tenants like it that way."

What did she think he was going to do? Crash the joint with a six-piece marching band? She'd mentioned the quiet aspect a few times in her conversation with Liam. She had also apparently gone on about the teak furniture in her home. After reassuring her that Mike was a quiet man, Liam had reminded her he was coming to Honolulu to search for his brother.

"When he's not out looking for him, he'll be working on

his laptop in his room. He's a mystery writer and he's on a deadline."

Her response had been, "But the desk is teak."

Neither man knew what that meant and Liam had been unable to question her further. She'd taken a call on her other line and said simply, "Tell Mike to call me when he gets here."

She'd made a passing reference to her teak furniture again in her message. If only he hadn't paid for the room in advance. Now Mike wished he had insisted on a hotel room. He wanted to grab something to eat, shower, and sleep. On the other hand, he kept telling himself, since it would have put him in debt, staying with a local could mean that he might be able to ask for advice and bounce ideas around when he needed it.

"Is that your stomach rumbling?" Keanu's warm voice interrupted his thoughts.

"It's nothing," Mike said, surprised to hear it himself.

"Alvin told me you threw up earlier. Sounds like you're dehydrated and you need a good meal. I know just the place. Not many are open late on the island, but this place has good food and comfy booths. We can talk until your crazy landlady calls."

"How do you know she's crazy?"

Keanu shot him a sheepish grin as he stopped for a light. "I couldn't help hearing her voice on your phone. She mentioned teak in her message. Who obsesses about their furniture when they're renting out rooms in their home? And forgive me, but I am always suspicious of *haole* who move to the islands and give themselves woo-woo names. They're usually bat-shit crazy."

Mike actually laughed. The guy had her pegged all right. "Is *haole* a derogatory term for tourists?"

Keanu gave him an appreciative grin. "You learn fast."

Mike wondered about something. "When did you talk to

Alvin?"

"I called him to see if it was okay for me to come to the house."

"Oh, all right." Mike thought a moment. "You know those officers well?"

"I went to Punahou, which is a very good school here, with Noah. And I went through the police academy with Alvin."

"You didn't become a police officer?"

Keanu was silent a moment. "Yeah, I did. I don't work for them anymore."

The rumbling in Mike's stomach interrupted their conversation.

"You *are* hungry,"

"Not really."

"Yes, really." Keanu gave him an appraising glance.

"What?"

"You're allowed to eat, you know. Luca needs you healthy and strong. You need your strength and I know just the place. It's right off Lunalilo Home Road, so we'll be nice and close for when she's ready."

"I need to get my car."

"We'll pick it up in the morning. I'll come get you and take you there. By then we might have some new information."

Mike said nothing. He was tired, but so grateful that this private investigator seemed to care. A small niggle began at the back of his mind. *I hope he doesn't think I'm going to pay him. I don't have that kind of money.*

Keanu pulled left off the highway into a massive outdoor complex called the Koko Marina Mall. Through a maze of mostly closed businesses, including a Starbucks and a Walgreens drug store, they pushed through to the back and parked outside a restaurant with a sign saying *Zippy's*.

They trooped up the few short stairs to the entrance, into an airy takeout section that had a roof but was otherwise open to the elements. They passed this to a comfortable and warm dining section. The smiling waitress greeted them and led them to a booth by the windows. The breeze seemed to have picked up into a full tropical wind, judging by the now-bent palm trees swaying in the wind. Rain began lashing the windows.

"It'll stop in a minute. It's always like this here," Keanu said, opening his menu. From somewhere, The Carpenters song *Rainy Days and Mondays* tinkled across the room.

"What is that body of water out there?" Mike gazed out at the boats moored outside a couple of swanky-looking homes.

"Those are remnants of ancient Hawaiian fish ponds. Once upon a time, Hawaii Kai was nothing but one gigantic fishpond that belonged to the royal family. The monarchy was overthrown just before the turn of the nineteenth century, but the ponds remained in use until, of course, developers got their hands on it. Almost all the construction here is on top of the remains of those sacred ponds. This is all that's left, and it won't be developed, thank God."

In the distance, Mike spotted what looked like a volcanic crater. "I'm all turned around. Is that Diamond Head?"

"No, that's Koko Head, the other extinct crater on the island. There are some marvelous hiking trails up there."

Mike took a deep breath, wondering if his brother had found his way up any of those trails.

The waitress appeared and, after some brief suggestions from Keanu, Mike chose the mahi mahi plate and some iced tea.

"Have a Coke," Keanu advised. "No ice. It will help settle your stomach."

He's right. I should have thought of that. I just can't think straight right now.

As the waitress left with their orders, Mike said, "The place my brother went to, the Pali, is that a common hiking trail?"

"Oh, yes." Keanu leaned both elbows on the table and sipped at the iced water that had magically appeared. He seemed to be gathering his thoughts. "There are some beautiful but very isolated trails up there. There are even secret tunnels. Most of these you will never find in a guide book, but for the people who truly love these islands and the wild aspects of the nature here, the Pali holds an allure that is captivating, but sometimes . . . dangerous."

Mike grimaced. "That sounds like my brother. He's one of those off-the-beaten-path kind of guys."

The waitress returned with their drinks. Mike soon saw that Keanu liked his iced tea heavily sugared.

"With the Pali, because it's only a few miles away from civilization, people don't think of it as even remotely perilous," Keanu said, taking a deep slug of his tea. He gave a quick glance to Mike. "Sorry."

"Don't apologize. What's so dangerous? As far as I know, there are no deadly snakes or venomous spiders. I've heard you have wild pigs in the mountains—"

"We have a few spiders, and scorpions. And yes, feral pigs. It's none of those. Frankly, it's human beings I worry about. We're playing unwilling host to an increasing number of homeless people."

"Really? Are things that tough in the islands?"

Keanu sighed. "Don't get me started. Yes, things are tough."

"That cop, Noah, told me that missing people aren't a big problem in the islands. Is that true?"

Keanu looked stunned. "That was a bald-faced lie. People go missing every day here. Locals and tourists. We have the highest rate of unsolved murders in the whole of the US. And—" he held u a hand, "We have an inexplicable amount of wanted felons hiding in plain sight."

"So, you have your work cut out for you as a P.I." Mike sipped his Coke through a straw. The uneasiness in his stomach abated.

"I'm busy with a lot of family requests for missing people. Mostly kids. Once teenagers reach the age of seventeen here, even if I find them, I can't force them to contact home. But, I give them burner phones with enough money on them to make a call if and when they feel like it."

"That's good of you."

Keanu shrugged. "It's part of my fee." He lapsed into a troubled silence.

"So, people like my brother aren't that unusual."

"Not really, no. The islands are geared toward tourism. So, some people who choose to live here are doing well, while others struggle. I know people who are holding down two and three jobs just to stay in paradise. It takes a strong mind to make a go of it here. It really does."

Mike thought fleetingly of Kelly Park and how she'd rented out rooms, with her situation getting out of control. He sipped his Coke and the tangy, familiar sweetness soothed his ragged soul. In his first year of chemistry, he'd learned that the taste of Coca-Cola was all in people's heads. Something about the combination of the chemicals and sugars triggered a sense of nostalgia in the human psyche. You could ask six people what Coke tasted like and you'd get six different responses.

"The problem is the hardworking people who lose their homes because in the last four years prices have skyrocketed here," Keanu said. "When Obama became president, tourists flocked to the islands to see the place where he was born. It resurrected our sagging economy and then some. It gave hotels and condo owners who rented out their properties permission to price-gouge. If you don't know the history of our islands, then you will discover that this is how we lost control of our home the moment Western explorers set foot here."

"I heard AirBnB was banned on Oahu, which was why I was forced to find something on Craigslist. I can't afford the hotels here."

Keanu gave him an odd look. "That wasn't the best decision the state ever made. A lot of elderly people relied on the income renting out a room or an apartent on AirBnB and HomeAway brought them. It was a bill designed to help the skyrocketing hotel room prices."

"Do you think the other islands will ban AirBnB too?"

"There's already a ripple effect. I hope not, to be honest. We have an icreasing number of what we call unsheltered homeless on the islands. Some of this population is right here in the tourist mecca. There's also a one-point-seven-mile stretch of beach in Makaha, well away from the tourists, that's called Tent City. Filled with homeless families."

"I think I saw it on *Dog the Bounty Hunter*."

"Right. He took his life into his own hands going there at night, but under cover of darkness it's easier to catch criminals unaware. By night, most of the guys start drinking and then the fights begin. Since Dog's wife died, he's not so active now. I think he's in Colorado mostly."

Keanu took another sip of tea. "Our biggest problem is the hordes of white-collar criminals released from the Pacific Northwest prisons. They're given one-way tickets to Maui and Honolulu. They've brought rampant theft and prolific drug use here. We can't get rid of 'em."

"I had no idea." Mike's spirits sank to his shoes. His brother had rhapsodized about his dreams of a Hawaiian life. Surely all this human misery wasn't part of Luca's fantasy.

Keanu nodded. "Most of them wind up homeless. If you went down to Kalakaua Avenue right now, that's the main street of Waikiki, you'd see them on the sidewalks, panhandling and harassing the tourists. It's become such a nightmare the cops now spend their time canvassing the sidewalks, offering the homeless a room for a night in a nice hotel, a hot meal, a bath, and a plane ticket back to their homes on the mainland."

"Do they get a lot of takers?"

"Not as many as they'd like. Some people want to hold on to the illusion of paradise in the Pacificeddo."

"Is it an illusion?" Mike looked up from his drink to hold Keanu's gaze.

"Some days I believe it is. There are things about this place that I love. It's the human element, the unknown danger, I worry about."

"I never see this side of the island on *Hawaii Five-O*," Mike said.

"Oh, my God. That show." Keanu looked pained. "It has no resemblance to reality. I mean, the guys are hot, I'll give you that, but they get in their car on one side of the island and two seconds later they're on another side entirely. In one episode, they even managed to drive to a whole different island!"

Mike laughed. This was his first inkling that Keanu was gay, and for some reason it gave him hope. *Stop it. You're being stupid.*

"Speaking of cars, he said, "I'm curious, since you're a local, why you're renting one.

Keanu blushed. "I blew up the engine of mine. Forgot to put oil in it. I was doing surveillance work at the time, following a cheating husband. I absolutely blew my cover when my vehicle exploded." He chuckled. "It's been in the shop for weeks."

Mike would have responded but their waitress returned with steaming plates. Mike was pleased to discover how fresh and flavorful the mahi-mahi was. The portions were generous and he devoured his side salad and scoop of macaroni salad quickly. He tried not to stare when Keanu poked his finger into his mashed potatoes and sucked it. He managed to make it seem so erotic. *Damn.*

The waitress returned and refilled Mike's Coke. He needed

the distraction. "Thanks," he said.

She gave him a dazzling smile, though her focus seemed to be the handsome Keanu and, as she walked away, Mike realized he and Keanu had been eating in companionable silence.

"Good food, isn't it?" Keanu had eaten as quickly as he had.

"Very good. So tell me, what other kind of cases do you get as a private investigator here? You mentioned a cheating husband and missing teens."

Keanu forked some salad. "I've had a few interesting cases. A missing painting. A missing dog. A missing chicken." Another chuckle. "But I deal with the homeless population a lot."

"Really?" Mike shook his head. "I seem to be saying that a lot since I got here. What is it that you do for the homeless people?"

"Well, I have clients on the mainland looking for family members. Relocating here for many of the people who have been formerly incarcerated is really living off the grid. It's fatal for some of them. Many of them drift to the beach until the police shoo them away. Some then go into hiding in the mountains, eating fruit and taking drugs and, one day, they disappear. The hills are full of these people who've gone plum crazy. They take up pockets of land and believe it's theirs and can become quite . . . combative if somebody stumbles across their little patch of turf. I'm more worried about those people than the feral pigs, quite frankly."

Mike shivered and dropped his fork on his plate. "You think it's possible my brother came across one?"

"Anything's possible, but he may not be there at all. He might have staged the scene."

Mike thought for a moment. It was feasible, very much so. He mentioned Luca's backpack being left behind.

"See." Keanu pointed a finger at him. "That shows me that he didn't just disappear. He staged things."

"You've seen it before."

Keanu nodded. "Yes, I have. I've helped a few families locate their loved ones. I just had a case last week. A pair of elderly parents told me their son was a chronic drunk, in and out of jail. He was sent here from Seattle, Washington. They didn't expect him to come back to the mainland but they also wanted to know he was okay. They sent me a cell phone for him loaded with a lot of minutes. He's one of the few who's willing to call his family once a week to let them know he's okay."

"Wow. That's amazing. They're not worried he'll sell it?"

"No. It has iTunes for music, and Netflix, so he can watch movies and TV shows. He's thrilled to have that bit of normalcy. He guards that phone like a jewel. He charges it up at the library or over at Starbucks. They also sent money to me to keep a small tab for him at the local Foodland store. He can go in and get food and drinks, but no cash."

"His parents sound like remarkable people."

"They are." Keanu seemed suddenly emotional. "They have accepted him for who he is. They can live peacefully knowing he can reach out if he wants to and he has me for backup if he ever feels the need."

"They pay you for that?"

He didn't respond.

Mike suspected keanu had taken on some of the responsibility for this man out of the goodness of his heart. "You're a really decent man, Keanu."

"Thank you. I take my work seriously. I don't like to see people suffering. I'm a pretty good human bloodhound. I'd like to help you find your brother."

Ah, there's the rub. "I can't pay you," Mike said, expecting the guy to walk out on the spot.

"I didn't ask you to. I have tomorrow free, then I start a new case." He blew out a breath. "Actually, it's taking up a case I already worked on I feel has nowhere to go." He shrugged. "So let me show you some island hospitality and maybe I can help."

Wow. So this was the aloha spirit. "What is the case you feel has no place to go?"

Keanu stared at his food a moment. "A missing teen. Local. Gone four years now. I was on the force when he first vanished from his bedroom. I saw him. I saw that kid and couldn't convince him to go home. He was a few days away from being sixteen. His parents still miss him."

"What do you think happened to him?"

Keanu shook his head. "Dead, probably."

Silence fell between them.

"Dead?"

"He was in a treacherous place with kids he shouldn't have been with, camping on a rock by a dangerous surf break. I'm pretty certain he drowned. He didn't have the tools to survive so long on his own." Keanu's eyes seemed wounded as his voice dropped to a whisper. "That's why I'd like to help you. This case is fresh."

Mike was so overcome with gratitude he didn't know what to say. The waitress brought the check and he grabbed it. "Let me buy you dinner at least."

"That, you can do." Keanu grinned at him.

Mike glanced at the check, surprised to see it was under twenty dollars. Liam had squawked about the high island restaurant prices. He put down his credit card. He didn't mind paying for the meal. Besides, Keanu seemed like a nice guy. Liam would have a fit when the charge showed up.

So what. It's my card. And I let him charge all those business expenses to it and he never reimbursed me, then we lost our company. Enough now. Don't think about it.

He forced himself not to dwell on the subject of the dreams he and Liam had shared. Mike had given up a steady, lucrative position as a pharmacist to open the café. It had all gone wrong, horribly wrong.

That's probably why I was so hard on Luca chasing his dreams here. I was afraid he'd fail. I didn't want to see him get hurt. I'm sorry I didn't fight harder to stop him, but I was afraid of losing him. Now I really might have lost him. Permanently.

Mike tried taking a couple of deep breaths. The panic that was always so close to the surface for him these days flared again. He tried not to think of his brother lying at the bottom of a ditch somewhere. Or drowning in violent surf.

"You okay?" Keanu asked as Mike's cell phone rang. Serenity was around the corner. They made arrangements to meet her further up Lunalilo Home Road, in the parking lot of the local library.

"You can't miss me," she said. "I have a little brown car, the color of pooh, and one taillight is missing."

Pooh. Lovely.

He paid the check and when he walked outside with Keanu, he noticed that the rain had stopped. In fact, it looked like there had been no downpour at all. They drove up the hill and found Serenity waiting in the parking lot as promised.

She flashed her lights and waved. Mike caught a glimpse of a blonde, bouffant hairdo and kept his sights on it as Keanu kept following her up a maze of tall, narrow, winding streets that went for about three miles.

"I've lived here all my life and never had occasion to come up here," Keanu muttered. "I think I just got nosebleed."

Mike kept staring out the window. He could see long, low-roofed houses, a park, and beyond this, open spaces. Serenity turned left without warning, and Keanu followed her. She finally pulled into a very dark parking lot and leaned out of her window, pointing to a space on her left.

"Park there," she shouted.

Keanu obeyed, pulling into a tiny guest parking space between a thorny bush and some stinky garbage bins.

"I didn't know there were going to be two of you," she

grumped when Keanu and Mike got out of the car.

"I'm not staying. I just brought him here." Keanu stuck his hand out and introduced himself. "I'm Keanu Māhoe, this is Mike deCosta."

Mike was trying to recover from the fact that the woman had the deepest tan he'd ever seen in his life. He could tell this even from the very dim light thrown from an apartment beside them. She was slim, long-legged and possessed of the bright blonde hair women of a certain age tended to favor. In spite of her tiny, short shots and halter top she wasn't any carefree sprite. She was at least sixty and not in a very good mood.

"I told you guests weren't allowed," she told Mike with a frosty stare.

Boy. So far she is not living up to her name.

CHAPTER FOUR

"I'm not visiting. I'm dropping him off. I'm a private investigator here in Honolulu. I'm helping Mike look for his missing brother."

"Oh." She blinked a couple of times, as though not quite sure how to compute this information.

Keanu retrieved Mike's suitcase and laptop bag from his trunk. "I'll walk you to your door, then I'll split."

Mike nodded, suddenly wishing Keanu would stay. He had a bad feeling about this landlady. He fell into stride beside Keanu with a now-babbling Serenity leading the way.

"This is our pool." She waved to the right. Mike spotted the most unappealing body of water he'd ever seen. It looked murky. He didn't think he'd be spending any time in it. They reached her door and he realized she lived in a condominium. The place was shrouded in darkness and when she flicked on a light, he saw wall-to-wall tacky furniture and fake flowers in gigantic floor pots.

Yuck.

At least there were no drugged-out kids on mattresses.

"Please take your shoes off," she said. "No shoes in the house." Keanu had already kicked his off. Mike removed his.

"I'd prefer them to stay outside the house, but if you must bring them in, leave them there, just inside the door," Serenity said, looking miserable when Mike did just that.

He had no idea why she posted photos of her living room on Craigslist since she mentioned as soon as they walked inside that he'd have no access to it.

"This is a quiet unit. We must have complete silence at all times," she said.

"Seriously?" Keanu looked stunned.

She fixed him with a venomous look as she showed Mike his room. He immediately became depressed when he saw how tiny it was. Keanu put the laptop on top of the bureau and she went berserk, hurling the bag to the bed.

Mike and Keanu exchanged looks as Keanu set the small suitcase on the floor.

"Teak," she said, running her hand across the top of the bureau. "You can't watch TV, not that there's one in here. And I prefer you to keep the bedroom door open during the day. I like things nice and open in the day."

"And quiet," Keanu reminded her.

"Of course," she said, not noticing the twinkle in his eye.

She rabbited on and proceeded to take Mike upstairs to show him the bathroom.

"Why did you book this place?" Keanu grabbed his arm and whispered in his ear.

"I didn't. My ex did."

"He hate you or something?"

Serenity was watching them from the top of the stairs.

Mike had the urge to say, "Don't go," but he didn't.

He let Keanu escape, relieved when the PI told him he'd pick him up at seven o'clock in the morning to take him to the rental car agency. Mike watched him leave, feeling claustrophobic in this condo. He could tell already that the landlady had a good relationship with cleaning products, judging by the smell of furniture polish and bleach. And at least she was using them for the right reasons, not to cook up drugs.

As he followed her up the stairs, he wished she would turn on another light. She did, a small nightlight in the bathroom, but even that couldn't stop him from bumping into unfamiliar objects.

She fussed around for a moment, handing him a towel to use, giving him instructions to hang it in his bedroom closet, then finally left him alone. "You can store things in the fridge downstairs," she told him, "But you can't cook or use the stove."

No, of course not. Probably made of teak.

He used the restroom, then went back down to his room where he found her unabashedly going through his things.

He gasped. "What are you doing?"

"Checking for drugs and alcohol. "

"I don't have either. Now please, leave."

She brushed past him and he took a few moments to simmer down. He wondered what Keanu was doing now and imagined him halfway home to wherever that was, to be followed by a night in front of the TV with a beer.

I've never felt so lonely in my life.

He had to unwedge the huge, fluffy rug from the entrance to his room and flung it against the wall. He closed the door behind him, took his toiletries and a clean pair of shorts up to the bathroom, where he took a quick shower and brushed his teeth.

When he came back down, the bedroom door was open again!

She'd put the rug back in the doorway, lowered his blinds and turned down his bed. If he hadn't noticed a lock on the door he would have walked out immediately.

He turned the lock and fell into bed, his toothpaste and brush still in the grip of his tired fist.

Mike slept badly. Images of his brother rolling in foamy surf just out of reach, then beckoning him from deep inside a cave made him sweat. He awakened with the strange sensation of being unable to breathe. He took deep gusts of breath, but the air in the room was stale. He got out of bed and moved to the window. Pulling aside the vertical blinds, he saw that the windows were jalousies, with thick, horizontal slats and a crank-type handle. He turned the ancient crank until he managed to get the slats open about an inch.

Chill, damp air greeted him. He inhaled, grateful for the very faint tang of salt on the breeze, reminding him he was on an island. It was still too dark outside to see anything, but it sure was quiet.

He crawled back into bed and a few minutes later, heard a strange slapping sound. He bolted upright again. It was the vertical blinds reacting to the breeze.

Seconds later came a knock at the door. Oh, no. Serenity.

"Mike!" she whispered. "Too much noise!"

She knocked a few more times, then tried to force open the door.

Unbelievable. He didn't care what it cost, tomorrow he was getting out of here.

He closed the window and lay on the bed in the too-warm room. His body was slick with night sweats. He hadn't had them for a long time and wished they hadn't started now. He closed his mind to thoughts of his parents, who had caused his stress in the first place.

I've tried hard to look out for Luca. I haven't done a very good job.

Emotion welled in him. He shoved the sheets down to the bottom of the bed with his feet and heard Serenity retreating, finally. Mike closed his eyes. He had no idea what time it was and checked his cell phone. Four A.M. No surprise really. It was seven back home in LA. He would be getting up by now making his first pot of coffee. He longed for some now, but knew he couldn't make any in the kitchen.

He flipped on the bedside lamp and picked up the toothpaste and brush that had fallen to the floor. He shoved them into his laptop bag and retrieved his cell phone and earbuds. He scrolled through his iTunes library. Luca had given him a massive collection of 1970s era songs and Liam had downloaded them for him.

Luca and Liam. At one time, he'd hoped they could be the family he and Luca so craved. Both men were a part of Mike's story. He was a part of theirs. With Luca, he wanted more than anything for their shared story to continue. With Liam . . . He lay back against the pillows and realized that for him the final chapter had been written.

He received notification of a text message and checked, his pulse racing. He hoped it would be news from Luca. No such luck.

A sappy note from Liam. *I miss you. I want you back. Can't we try again?*

Mike ignored the text. He thought it was apt that the song he went back to in his shuffled playback was *It's Too Late*. Ha! Carole King knew what she was talking about.

He closed his eyes and tried to sleep. He knew it would be a long day and he needed to get as much rest as possible. The song changed.

Sky High, by the British group, Jigsaw. Just like the guy in the song, Liam had blown it all sky high with his lies.

That could have been Mike and Liam's anthem. It *was* too late and Liam had ruined it all.

For some reason, *Rainy Days and Mondays* came on next. He had no idea the song was even in his rotation. Mike pulled out the earbuds, turned off the music and rolled over. Tears fell from his eyes. Why had he and Luca been dealt such a rough hand in life? They were good people. They worked hard, and loved hard.

I am going to find him. I'm going to be the best brother he ever had again. Please God, give me another chance.

He lay, thoughts of the past tumbling into his mind. He had to be strong. He had to stop. He sat up on the bed, anxious to run, walk, do something. Anything other than spend another moment in this tiny, suffocating room. But he was spent. Body and soul. He forced himself back down to the bed. He closed his eyes once more and this time he fell asleep, way too tired to even reach across and turn off the bedside lamp.

Mike awoke a few hours later with a start.

Somebody was slamming a vacuum cleaner against his door. Serenity. What the hell was wrong with the woman? He checked the time on his cell phone. Six forty-seven in the morning. He remembered that Keanu would be picking him up at seven. Out of habit, he tried calling Luca's cell phone. Previously his calls had gone straight to voice mail. Now he reached a recording saying the messages were full.

He also tried Greg's cell phone but the call went straight to voicemail. He quickly plugged in his laptop but realized he didn't have a WiFi access code and shut it down again. He went online via his cell phone, checking for any reports of his brother.

One lone item appeared in the Honolulu Star-Advertiser.

Mainland Tourist Vanishes

Witnesses who watched a Northern California man get sucked into a Maui blow hole to his apparent death say the tourist was dancing around and frolicking in the sprays of water seconds before a wave knocked him down.

Mike let out a sigh. It wasn't his brother. He ran a hand through his hair. There was nothing about his brother. The only references to Luca were his Facebook and Twitter pages. Neither had been updated for days. He'd checked the previous morning and now, he wished for something, anything, even his brother's goofy 'What's your porn name' posts.

He checked Greg's Instagram account, the only social networking site he used. Officially, anyway. He'd posted a photo of himself near Diamond Head with the caption, *Living the good life. Just another day in paradise.*

Greg looked kinda rough in the photo, but maybe his three-day growth was supposed to be sexy He looked thin and

48

hollow-eyed, a typical tweaker for sure.

Mike wished the guy was right here in front of him. He'd punch his lights out and send him to a different kind of paradise.

He sighed again and got offline. He badly wanted a shower, but when Mike gathered his things together and raced upstairs, the bathroom was occupied. From the cracked-open door, he could see a tall blonde woman standing in front of the mirror blowdrying her hair in an almost hypnotic way.

Good luck if you're in a hurry for a shower, which I am. He paced the small space outside the door. The woman kept up her languid hairdressing speed. Is she kidding me? It's Waikiki! It's the beach!

Serenity appeared with a rag and a bottle of cleaning fluid. She'd come to snoop under guise of taking care of things. *Oh, brother.*

"I can let you know when the bathroom's free," she said.

"I'm in a hurry. I really need to get in there," he said.

The blowdryer droned on.

"There's a half-bathroom downstairs," she said.

He sprinted away from her and hurried into the tiny space before she'd even finished her sentence. He once again brushed his teeth, washed his face, and hoped Serenity wouldn't have a fit that he'd moved her cheap, fake, fluffy rug aside to close the bathroom door. Keeping an ear out for Keanu, he gave himself a sponge bath and felt much better by the time he'd thrown on a fresh T-shirt and board shorts and returned to his room. That was, until he saw Serenity in the doorway, bending down to put his rug back in position.

Mike resisted the strong desire to kick her ass. Instead, he said, "I need to change, Serenity, I'm not doing it with the door wide open."

He could see now that she'd also made his bed and opened

his blinds. Man, he really had to get the hell out of here. He shoved aside the rug and was shocked to find Keanu sitting on his bed.

"Good morning," the tall Hawaiian said, an amused look on his face.

Oh, man.

"No visitors," Serenity said.

"He came to pick me up, We won't be long," Mike said with as much politeness as he could muster. He knew when he closed the door she would be out there listening. He hadn't had a chance to unpack, which was a good thing, but where would he go? He wouldn't think about it now. He'd get what he needed for the day. With a glance out the window, he saw that nobody was outside. He yanked open the bedroom door and there she was, a glass in her hand, ear to what had been hollow wood.

She straightened.

He didn't want to stay here, but he had no desire to start hunting for new accommodations.

"This the house key?" Keanu asked, rising from the bed and dipping into a glass dish on the bedside table.

Mike glanced at Serenity, who nodded. Keanu handed it to him. Mike packed what he needed into his laptop bag and slung it over his shoulder. He left everything else in his suitcase, which he locked and stowed in the closet.

He knew as he and Keanu left that she would be putting the rug back in the doorway again.

Outside the condo, Mike and Keanu put their shoes back on. They could see her maniacally cleaning through Mike's bedroom windows.

"Teak!" she shrieked as she rubbed at Mike's bedside table.

Boy, was she a loon.

The two men exchanged amused glances, but it was not until they were in his car and heading down the mountain that Keanu said, "She's a trip and a half, isn't she?"

"You've got no idea."

"No visitors!" Keanu mimicked and they both laughed. "What are you going to do? You can't stay there." Keanu seemed genuinely concerned as they wound down toward the highway.

"I'll find a hotel room later. I'm anxious to get going. Any news on my brother? I looked online and there are no reports on him. I should have checked with the local hospitals in case he turned up there—"

"He's not in any hospitals. The police checked. Greg's okay by the look of things. He posted a photo on Instagram that made my blood boil."

"I saw it, too, and had the same reaction." Mike shook his head. "His boyfriend, the alleged love of his life, goes missing and he doesn't give a crap."

"Apparently so." Keanu paused at a red light. "Look, the police have circulated your brother's photo to every single precinct on the island. They've also sent it to all the hotels and hostels, and the airport here in Honolulu. There are ways around the AirBnB ban, apart from brave people who advertise on Craigslist. There's a bunch of hostels and shared rooms available in Waikiki. I started putting the word out about your brother. I took the liberty of snatching his Facebook profile pic and emailing it to the people I know who rent out cheap places."

"Wow. That's amazing. Thanks."

"Ain't no big t'ing." Keanu seemed to have lapsed into island speak as they loitered at a red light.

"Can we stop at a Drive-thru? I need coffee and something to eat."

Keanu lifted a brow. "We'll have breakfast soon, but I could use a coffee, too. Hold on." He swerved across three lanes of traffic into a McDonalds driveway. Cars skidded to stop but he didn't earn a single honk.

Mike treated them both to coffee and they were on their way again.

"The police have informed the local paper and something will come out today," Keanu said, swinging his coffee in his free hand. "I found that out when I dropped by the police station at Diamond Head just before I came to get you."

"Thank you. That's good to know."

"They've been working hard on this case. It's bad for business when tourists vanish."

"Yeah. I read about the guy in Maui that got sucked into a blow hole."

"Can you believe it? We warn people that Mother Nature is beautiful but deadly. His whole family watched him get sucked into the hole. He apparently bobbed back up for a second and then another wave just crashed right into him."

Mike winced. "They haven't found the body?"

"Nope. Not likely to either. He's gone." He flicked a glance at Mike. "That doesn't mean your brother got hit by a wave. Listen, we'll be meeting up with Detective Ng very soon. He told me the park rangers did a cursory search of the tourist spots up on the Pali Lookout yesterday. They've searched as far as they can of the immediate drop area below the Lookout's platform, but there's no sign of him."

"Will they keep searching there?"

"It's difficult. It's completely undeveloped terrain. No marked trails, no paths, nothing. Two hundred years ago when King Kamehameha the Great conquered the island of Oahu, he forced the defeated king's vanquished warriors to take their own lives by jumping off the Pali into the depths below."

"My God! And they did it?"

"Yes. And a couple of years ago, construction workers who'd gone all the way down to check via cranes that the Pali Lookout's foundations were sturdy, made a few gruesome discoveries. They found human skulls that, turns out, date back to that time. They've been there all these years."

Mike was silent for a moment. "Okay, what next?"

"Well, I've organized a search party, but we start at nine. I thought we'd grab some coffee and eggs, and we can go over some things."

"Sure, that sounds great." *You're such a nice guy Keanu. I want to trust you, but I'm trying to figure out why you're being so kind to me.*

It took them twenty minutes in the snarled morning traffic to reach the highway and head toward Waikiki. Mike stared out at the amazing view. He hadn't realized how picturesque Hawaii Kai had been, driving there in the dark. They jumped on the freeway. Rain spattered the windows, but they made it to Waikiki, where everything looked dry.

The main center of the island of Oahu appeared to be a maze of one-way streets. The traffic, the noise, and the countless pedestrians all made Mike yearn for the um, serenity of Hawaii Kai.

Keanu found street parking on the tiny Saratoga Road, right off the main drag of Kalakaua Avenue. Mike was confused by the parking signs, which were unlike any he'd seen before.

"They're designed to be that way. Trust me, HPD counts on people goofing up. Parking tickets are their bread and butter." Keanu showed him how the car had to be parked right between two white lines. Any stray piece of bumper over the line would cost a minimum of sixty dollars in fines.

They were still ahead of the eight o'clock meter-starting time, but Keanu threw quarters in anyway. Mike looked up and down Saratoga. Most of it seemed taken up by the Trump International Hotel Waikiki, which commanded stunning views of the ocean on one side and other hotels' jammed courtesy buses on the other. Tourists pummeled the pavement and other pedestrians. Squeezed between the Trump and a series of smaller hotels was an ABC shop. Mike had lost count of the number of those he'd seen between here and Hawaii Kai. And nestled between all this activity was an inviting-looking restaurant called Eggs N Things.

Judging by the crowd, it was very popular.

"This isn't even the busy time yet," Keanu said, obviously sensing Mike's apprehension. He waved a hand at a long table inside filled with chattering people. "These aren't tourists, by the way, this is your brother's search party."

Mike couldn't believe it. He swallowed over the lump in his throat. All these wonderful people. Here. To help him find Luca.

Keanu's eyes darted in every direction, typical cop that he was. They grabbed a small table for two and pushed it toward the others.

Keanu introduced Mike to everybody. He tried to keep track of all the names. Down at the end of the table was Detective Ng, who was supposed to be the man to call upon his arrival.

The detective brought his coffee and toast over to them and introduced himself.

"Call me Sam. Sorry I wasn't available last night. Been a busy few days."

"Please, don't apologize."

As the waiter took Keanu and Mike's orders, other people in their group began eating. Mike was stunned that three detectives from a different precinct, a nurse, a doctor, two firemen, and a hula teacher had all chosen to spend their free days looking for a stranger.

Mike ordered coffee, scrambled eggs, macadamia pancakes, and, at Keanu's suggestion, sliced papaya drizzled with fresh lime.

As they waited for their food, Keanu unfolded a topographical map of the Pali and passed photocopies to everybody else.

"I've organized a couple more guys to help us look for Luca. One guy flies helicopters for an island tour. He's donating two hours of his time for the cause."

"Good one," Sam Ng said, raising his coffee cup in a toast.

Keanu spoke again and the table fell silent. "This is where Luca's rental car was found. Parked to the side of the Old Pali Road."

"So he wasn't at the Pali Lookout?" somebody asked.

"Doesn't look that way, but he may have walked. The thing is, Sam says his cell phone pinged down here." He pointed to a red dot farther down what looked like a highway.

Mike studied it. It looked at least a good mile from the Pali Lookout, not that it meant anything to him. Luca might have gone for a walk, but what was located at the area his cell phone had pinged?

When he asked Keanu, Sam answered.

"The cell phone company got a hit yesterday morning, but it faded. Nothing since. We sent a squad car there and two officers looked around. It's an unusual place to get a hit."

"Why?" Mike asked. "What's there?"

Keanu looked at him as the waiter slid their coffee cups onto the table. "Thanks," he acknowledged, flicking his gaze back to Mike. "The Consulate General of the Republic of Korea."

"That *is* unusual." Mike didn't know what to make of it.

"The police found nothing. Does your brother have any friends in the consulate?" Keanu asked.

"None that I know of."

Keanu nodded. "There are a few embassies and consulates in that area, but the pinging was very strong there."

"We looked, but there was no sign of your brother or his phone. And none of the staff recognized him from his photo," Sam said

"How do they have a photo of him?"

Sam hooked his thumb toward Keanu. "Also, his former landlady gave one to us. It was a candid snap Greg took."

Mike thought for a moment. "I don't mean to question your investigation, Sam, but let's just say for some strange reason my brother did go to the Korean Consulate General. It's sovereign soil, isn't it? If he felt endangered for any reason, wouldn't they be compelled to protect him?"

"He's not Korean," Sam pointed out. "And we're in America. Not the Middle East. Relations between our country, the state of Hawaii, and the Korean Consulate General are friendly. They wouldn't hold back information, especially when we've made it clear the young man has family looking for him."

"Okay, thanks." Mike gazed across the table and caught the sympathetic gaze of Quirinne, the hula teacher. He felt wretched and frightened for his brother. Where the hell could Luca be?

People started chatting again and Mike studied the map once more.

Keanu nudged him, his voice low. "By the way, I have some news on Greg, but haven't tracked him down yet. I spent some time online very late last night trying to get a lead on him. There's something you should know. He's all over the gay dating websites looking for a man."

"What? Are you kidding me?"

Keanu shook his head, his voice dropping even more. "He's looking for anyone with a place to stay, especially guys with money. I found him on the prowl on that hot new gay app, Scruff."

He took out his cell phone, pressed a few keys and handed it over to Mike, who was stunned to read:

Hey guys, I'm new in town. My boyfriend and I are looking for a 3sum. He likes to watch me, I like to watch him. Hit me up. We're 420 friendly.

"My God. How did you know to find him on this Scruff thing?"

"It's linked to his Instagram."

"I never noticed that." Mike stared at the ad. "He's trolling for dates while my brother is missing? And four twenty friendly. That's code for 'we like to get high' isn't it?"

Keanu nodded.

"How old is this ad?"

"A few days old, but he's had some hits, and he's responding. His latest messages to guys are that he and his boyfriend are both looking for a place to stay. He says they're desperate."

"How do you know this? Can you read his responses to people?"

Keanu blushed slightly. "Um, no. I posed as a rich guy looking for fun. I'm supposed to be meeting him at five o'clock for cocktails."

CHAPTER FIVE

Mike sat back in his chair, not sure of what to say. "Seriously?" he managed, just as the waiter brought their food. He didn't think he could eat now, and regretted ordering so much food.

"Eat," Keanu said. "You gotta keep your energy up. We may have no chance later. I have no idea when we'll get a bite again today. I've been thinking." He said this as he picked up his knife and slathered butter all over his pancake. "We should leave your rental at the Jensen parking lot for now. I'll take you there later, but you'd better call them and let them know. Now eat, my friend. We gotta hurry. We have to be on the road in fifteen minutes."

Keanu shoveled food down his jaw as though it were vital fuel.

Mike picked at his meal, but managed a second cup of coffee as thoughts flooded his mind.

"You're really going to meet him at five?" he asked, plucking macadamias out of his pancake.

"Of course. I already informed Alvin. He and Noah will give me back up and step in and apprehend him." He grinned suddenly. "Greg might be an ass, but he's got good taste in music. We're meeting at the Melissa Hotel to hear John Cruz performing. He's a really great Hawaiian musician."

That gave Mike some comfort. Maybe Greg would be forced to cough up what he knew.

What a pity that the rack has been outlawed. I would love to torture the truth out of that guy . . .

58

The ad really bothered him. "It just doesn't sound like my brother. He's a romantic, like me. He isn't the type to go looking for a threesome, or a rich guy."

"Does it sound like Greg?" Keanu asked.

"Yeah, unfortunately it does." Mike tried not to brood.

The waiter rushed over, bringing everybody's checks, and gave Mike a sweet smile. "Your breakfast is on the house. We all wish you much aloha and good luck finding your brother."

Mike thanked the man and left him a huge tip. Maybe he'd get to like this island after all . . .

He drove with Keanu once more, the others following in their carpooled vehicles. Mike made a quick call to the Jensen car rental agency and they let him know his car was safe, but he'd still be charged whether he drove the car out of there or not. He hadn't expected not to be charged.

With a pang, he remembered that Liam had texted him. He hadn't returned the message.

Being here gave him the freedom not to feel the need to jump every time Liam contacted him.

"You okay?" Keanu asked as they joined the flow of traffic onto the H1 Freeway. Within a few short stops he saw a sign saying *Pali Highway* and they left the freeway. It turned out to be a pretty, wide-spaced, verdant street with majestic trees on either side and a towering set of emerald green cliffs ahead of them.

"That's it. The Nu'uanu Pali," Keanu said.

"It's beautiful."

"Yes it is. It has quite a presence to it, in spite of its deadly history."

"Or maybe because of it," Mike remarked.

"Quite possibly. It's interesting that you say that. I have an uncle who conducts ghost tours of the island every night and he brings folk up here. All tourists of course. The other night I came because I had a date who wanted to go." He suddenly blushed. "Well, the guy freaked out when we got to the Pali Lookout."

"Why?"

"Well, I always thought Uncle's tours were a joke, but we stood at the lookout and I swear he was taking photos with his cell phone camera and all these blue dots floated across the screen. Uncle said they were paranormal ectoplasm. When the photo came out, we saw the distinct image of a young woman's face."

Mike stared at him. "For real?"

"Yeah. Killed the romantic mood."

For some reason this made Mike the happiest he'd been in days. Keanu was a sexy man. Definitely his type. Meeting under these circumstances was lousy as hell, but sheesh, if he had to be here searching for his missing brother, what a hot guy to be doing it with.

Mike experienced feelings of attraction he hadn't had for a long time. His cell phone rang and he clicked to receive his daily Rumi quote. He loved these spiritual nuggets but this one surprised him.

"What you seek is seeking you."
— Rumi.

How cryptic. Did this mean Luca, or was it referring to Keanu? Was he, too, yearning for a deeper connection with someone?

Don't be silly. It's just a quote. A quote for the day.

Right. But it's so apt.

"Think you'll see him again?" he asked Keanu.

"See who again?"

"Your date from the other night."

"Hell, no. He's not my type." He gave Mike the kind of glance that awakened Mike's cock in a way a full-on blowjob from Liam hadn't been able to achieve for a long, long, time.

He squirmed in his seat and concentrated on the view.

"My brother's cell phone pinged somewhere here, didn't it?"

"Yep. I'll show you."

Rain lashed the windows as they climbed the hill toward the mountain. Just as quickly, it stopped. Mike's cell phone rang. It was Sam Ng.

"I just talked to the man who drove your brother's rental car down from the Pali and he said he didn't notice anything suspicious. He just assumed the car was abandoned. He told me exactly where he found it though. It was on the Old Pali Road, not the Lookout as we first thought. I suggest we start there this morning."

"Okay," Mike said.

"If you pass the phone to Keanu, I'll tell him where to meet us."

Mike did as he was told.

"That's the Korean Consulate General," Keanu said, pointing to a huge white building to their left. A large property set back from the highway, it made Mike think of Southfork from the old *Dallas* TV series. Bordered by a long, low stone wall and surrounding hedge, a couple of tall cedars, and a few palms, it was not the imposing, impenetrable structure he had imagined.

He craned his neck to get a better look at it as they passed by, but all he could really tell was that it did have a big iron gate that wasn't open. The place didn't appear to be a fortress.

Keanu was deep in conversation with Sam when he suddenly said, "Hold on." He must have clicked over to the other line because he said, "Mike's phone. Yes, that's right. Can I tell him who's calling? Liam." He glanced at Mike. "I'll tell him. He's right here, but he'll need to get back to you. We're coordinating a search party right now and I have the detective in charge of the investigation on the other line."

Liam must have ended the call abruptly because Keanu raised his brows at Mike and shrugged.

Oh, there would be hell to pay when next Mike spoke to Liam. He just knew it. He fretted a little as they got closer to the mountains.

Keanu ended the call and handed the phone back to Mike. "Is Liam your boyfriend?"

"Ex. He's looking after my cat." Mike didn't want to get into any more details. It was already too much.

"How ex? He seemed irate that another man answered your phone. He hung up on me."

Mike swallowed. Hard. "He just moved out six weeks ago but it's been over for months. Longer than that even." He leaned his head back into the seat. "I should never have let it go on as long as I did."

"I had a relationship like that."

"You did?"

"Yeah. I quit the force because of him." There was deep sadness in Keanu's voice, but no anger.

"Why did you quit?"

"It was four years ago, right after the teenager who disappeared. That case really affected me. Then my love life took a weird turn. Being a gay cop in Hawaii isn't exactly . . . desirable. I worked hard to prove myself and Ray, my ex, well, he was a cop as well, and as soon as things went south between us he began stalking and harassing me." He glanced at Mike. "You don't want to hear all this. Too much drama."

"No. I want to know. To be honest, he sounds a lot like Liam."

"But you're letting him look after your cat."

"The cat is like my kid. Liam loved him, too, but when he moved out, I kept Herman. That's the cat's name. He's a great little kitty. I think I stuck it out for him, frankly."

Keanu laughed. "You're a softie."

"Yeah, I guess I am." He looked at Keanu. "So you left the force to get away from this guy?"

"I left after he made my life impossible. I got a transfer to the Big Island of Hawaii. I was stationed in Hilo but I missed being in a aplace with gorgeous sunsets."

"They don't have sunsets in Hilo?"

A soft smile, then, "No, they don't. Then I quit the force to become a private investigator. I heard Ray left the islands altogether, so here I am. It's been three years and I'm stalker free, and loving it."

Mike's cell phone rang. It was Liam.

A text.

I'm moving out and taking everything. Including the cat. Good luck with your new boyfriend. You didn't waste any time. Asshole.

Mike read and re-read the message. He didn't want Liam to take the cat. The truth was, they both wanted him. Whatever. Liam was going to make things difficult. He wasn't worried about Liam hurting Herman, but he knew he'd have to fight Liam to get him back. *I should have called Heidi. Damn.* She was willing to do it. He'd rescued Herman from the gutter and could prove it. He was the one who'd paid for all of Herman's vet bills.

See you in court, Liam.

As they neared the misty caps of the Pali's mountain peaks, it started to rain again. Big, fat drops fell on the windshield. The song *Rainy Days and Mondays* came to his mind. He'd never liked the rain, but now he hated it. They had to find his brother. How could they do that in the rain?

"Don't worry, this is another one of those tropical showers," Keanu said. "You like The Carpenters? *I love that song Rainy Days and Mondays.* I absolutely love the rain, don't you?"

The man was mad. Barking mad. Who could love the rain?

Mike regretted wearing shorts and a T-shirt.

"Rain is great. Makes everything smell so good. And look, landlubber, up there in the sky. A rainbow!" Keanu looked awed.

"Don't you see them all the time?"

"Yeah, but each one is different and this one's a sign of great good luck."

"Are you just saying that?"

"Of course not." Keanu looked offended. "We're a spiritual people here. We believe in signs and omens. A rainbow signifies good fortune."

"Good, I'll take it." Mike kept his eye on the road and noticed that the rain stopped as they turned onto the Old Pali Road. The street looked downright spooky with its heavy trees lining both sides and meeting in the middle. The cloud cover seemed so low Mike was certain that if he opened the window and reached up he could touch it.

Keanu drove until they approached what appeared to be an old water station.

"Luca left the car right there." Keanu tapped the window and pointed to a single parking spot outside of the green-colored building.

"Isn't that a strange place to park?" Mike asked.

"No. It depends on where he was headed. If he was parked here, I have no idea why the police searched the Pali Lookout, which we passed a few minutes ago. Parking here suggests he'd read something about one of the old trails that lead off from this road." Keanu waited a beat and said, "This is officially the middle of nowhere up here."

He pulled over to the right and parked as far off to the shoulder as he could. Bamboo trees lined both sides of the road, with huge trees overshadowing them in spaces. They got out of the car and Mike stretched, then looked around. Old, powdery bamboo disintegrated under his shoes leaving a fine layer of white dust on his ankles and footwear.

The others came up behind them, parking close as well.

"Make sure your cars are locked and no valuables are in sight," Sam instructed. "This is a bad area up here for theft."

Mike had trouble believing it 'up here in the middle of nowhere' but what did he know? His laptop was stowed safely in the trunk. He crossed the road, following Keanu who'd taken a piece of paper from Sam.

Keanu turned to Mike. "I see why the police searched the Pali Lookout. The report filed by the man who retrieved the rental car for Jensen indicated that's where he'd found it, but when Sam spoke to him last night, he clarified that the vehicle had been here."

The others had followed and were beginning to search the ground for clues.

"There's no obvious unmarked trail on this side, the popular ones are across the road," Keanu told him.

"What is this place? An old water pumping station?" Mike asked.

"Still in use. Part of the reason people park here is that it's very convenient to some unmarked, hidden trails. There's one about thirty feet ahead on the other side of the road that leads to Kaniakapupu."

"And what is that?"

"The ruins of King Kamehameha the third's summer palace. Not something you'll find in the official island guides but people still manage to find it. It's not a long or difficult hike but it is in the middle of a bamboo forest and it's considered sacred ground to us Hawaiians. We don't want people leaving trash or graffiti."

"We should go there now," Sam said, eyeing the sky. "The sun's coming out again. A quick prayer everyone."

That surprised Mike as much as the sudden sunburst. He joined hands with the others in a prayer circle.

The sun warmed his soul and his skin as Sam said, "We ask you, Father, for your help as we begin to search for Luca de-Costa today."

Mike blinked. It was still shocking to think of his brother as being . . . gone.

The group broke apart and a few more people appeared, including a police vehicle with two uniformed officers inside.

The officers emerged with a stack of *Missing* flyers. Mike felt a pang as he saw his brother's handsome face and his engaging smile. Luca was darker than Mike, his eyes more serious, in spite of his infectious grin.

Oh, Luca. Please come back to me.

Mike took a flyer and held it as everybody trooped up the road. There was no footpath but the Old Pali Road felt cool with the overhanging shade trees.

Just as Keanu had said, the entrance was unmarked but a significant hole between bamboo stems appeared to their right. Keanu led the way into the virtual tunnel of greenery.

The flash rain had left exposed bamboo roots and fallen leaves slick and slippery. A hush fell over the search party as the participants followed Keanu. He knew exactly where he was going and seemed oblivious to the others picking their way behind him. It became dark as they made their way, the trees seeming to close in on them. The air was fragrant however. Mike took a deep, appreciative breath. He thought about his stuffy night's sleep and hoped his brother was somewhere safe.

They trudged for a good half hour, taking turns here and there. There were so many ways to walk and Mike was grateful they had a guide. Keanu had them turning right as rain started to fall again, but Mike didn't care. He'd caught a glimpse of a building and they stepped forward into bright sunlight and the ruins of an old building.

Rain fell steadily now, but the day remained warm and

sunny. He was stunned by the beautiful incongruity of the natural splendor here.

He walked with Keanu and Quirinne. She split off with Sam, and the others spread out.

"Don't walk there," Keanu said, his tone soft as he pointed out a rectangular space filled with bright red plants. "That was where the ancient king did human sacrifices. The *kahuna* have come here and planted saplings to ease the *mana* of the place."

Mike swallowed. Human sacrifices. Oh, no. They covered the area, but there was no sign of Luca. Somebody found a discarded candy wrapper, but that didn't mean anything except whoever had dropped it was a litterbug.

They retraced their steps and covered other trails that shot off from the main one. The higher and deeper into the forest they went, the more the terrain changed. They hit a series of switchbacks, leaving the bamboo behind them. They began to encounter guava, jackfruit, ginger, and mango trees. Soon, the trees changed to Nepalese Elder and Norfolk Pine. It seemed staggering to find these in a Hawaiian habitat, but, Quirinne told him that most of the trees here were not indigenous.

"These mountains used to be filled with sandalwood trees, which the first Hawaiian kings traded with China and then the West for things like cannons, guns, ammunition, and building materials. They didn't plant replacement trees, and after thirty years of constant trading, they realized this was altering the eco-system. They sought bad advice and allowed foreign botanists to plant all these trees that have slowly strangled the native varieties. Most of what you see here, including the fragrant ginger and the papaya, is invasive."

Mike didn't know what to say to that. He kept walking, until the rain made things difficult and increasingly muddy. They reached a low point in the trail and had to climb under an old overpass covered in graffiti.

"I don't blame the tourists," Quirinne said. "I blame local kids. Some of them get bored and come out here and drink and desecrate. Sometimes these kids get rock fever real bad."

They stopped at one point and he was shocked to see the remains of a railway across the mountain range.

"There was a train that went around the whole island at one point," Quirinne told him. It disbanded in nineteen-forty-seven."

They passed a waterfall that had a few visitors. The two uniformed officers approached the tourists, handing out fly-ers with Luca's picture. Each of them shook their heads and the police returned to the group. Soon they came to a broken paved road. Mike learned it was the remains of the Old Pali Highway, that like the summer palace had not been looked after and the surrounding vegetation had consumed.

Mike and Keanu walked together. Mike realized he ex-pected his brother to jump out from the trees at any moment shouting "Gotcha!"

He pulled out his cell phone but had no reception. It was stupid to think Luca might have called him. He was surprised to see that it was one o'clock in the afternoon.

They wound up their search of the area, backtracking through a series of narrow switchbacks that left Mike a little nervous. In some parts, the trail was right on the edge of the cliffs. He had a serious fear of heights and couldn't look over.

Come to think of it, so did Luca.

"I don't think he came out here," he said, stopping to wipe the sweat from his brow. The heat of the day and all their ex-ertions had him out of breath. "Until we came to this spot I didn't think about it, but Luca wouldn't come to the edge of a precipice this way. We both have a fear of heights."

"Do you think he might have gone to the Pali Lookout?" Keanu asked, his gaze intense.

"I have no idea."

"It's pretty well protected with a railing. We could check."

Mike agreed. Keanu used a walkie-talkie feature on his cell phone to reach the other volunteers who'd taken different trails.

They all walked back to the road and met along the stretch of gravel where they'd parked.

Quirinne opened her trunk and removed chilled bottles of water she'd kept in a cooler. The grateful volunteers guzzled the refreshment, then headed in pairs to the Pali on foot.

Mike thought about his brother's movements. It was feasible that Luca might have gone to look at the ruins of the summer palace, which was nowhere near a cliff, and a short walk to boot, but—and it was a big but—Mike didn't think Luca, or anybody else could find it alone, unaided. Keanu had known where he was going and even he got turned around a couple of times. The trail veered off in many directions. It was possible they'd taken the wrong one, but with so many volunteers, a lot of ground had been covered.

"I want to search every inch of this island myself," Mike told Keanu as they walked back to the Pali. "I don't mean to sound ungrateful. I'm just so frustrated."

Keanu put a hand on his shoulder. "I hear you. I'd be feeling the same way you are if it were my brother. Hang in there, Mike. I have a good feeling about this one."

"You do?"

Keanu nodded. "I have sixth sense about these things. For example, I knew the date from the other night would turn out to be an idiot. I knew something was really worrying you the second I met you. I knew you were in a world of hurt. That was the only thing that stopped me from asking you out."

Mike smiled, really smiled, for the first time in two days. "When we find him, I hope you'll prove that to me."

"Don't worry. I will. Let's take this shortcut to the Pali from here." Keanu took his elbow and they cut through a thicket of trees just past the water station.

Mike was surprised to see a huge colony of feral kittens and a flock of black chickens co-existing along the trail once they reached it. Mike thought of his own cat with a pang. He would fight Liam every step of the way to get him back.

"This makes me so sad," Keanu said, bending down to stroke a kitten that was showing off for him, rolling around in the dirt. The kitten, though cute, turned out to be very skittish and darted off with his companions.

"Wait!" Mike shouted as the other felines followed. "There's a backpack between those plants."

Keanu bent down and, as the other volunteers joined them, he extracted the backpack. But it was very old and smelled really bad. Keanu held it away from him. "I don't even want to know what's inside this."

"Been there a long time," Sam said from behind Mike's right shoulder.

"It's not my brother's backpack anyway. I've got his back in my room."

They trudged forward, Sam questioning Mike about Luca's backpack.

When they reached the Pali Lookout, Mike understood finally what a massive drop it was from the cement platform to the vast expanse below. He thought about the king's vanquished warriors being forced to leap to their deaths.

The world was such a cruel place. Always was. Always would be.

He thought about the night he and Luka had learned their parents had staged a car accident, trying to kill them. They'd taken a life insurance policy on Luca and Mike. It had been devastating to know the parents who'd seemed so thoughtless and selfish all their lives were actually cold-blooded, calculating would-be killers. As he walked out onto the Pali and looked down on the untamed land tumbling all the way out toward the ocean, he wondered had those warriors been scared? Resolute?

Mike looked away, even though he knew he was safe behind the iron railing. He noticed a painting under a Perspex case over to his left. It was of the very scene he'd been thinking about and it was devastating to look at. Herb Kane, the artist, had an eye for detail. Each and every man's facial expression captured the horror of what was being done to them as they plunged into the abyss.

This was why he and Luca were afraid of heights. Their parents had drugged their meal one night during a supposed Hawaiian vacation. They'd packed Mike and Luca into a rented SUV and driven them to the edge of a cliff on the North Shore of Oahu. They had gotten out of the vehicle and plunged it over the embankment, but somehow Luca and Mike survived.

Mike had been the one to unbuckle Luca out of his stuck seatbelt. Even now, Mike could picture his terrified brother's silent, underwater scream. He'd dragged him to shore and waited. And waited. He'd finally waited until daylight when the police came with his parents, pretending to be panicked about their lost boys.

Mike told them everything. He and Luca had been taken away and their parents tried to convince a judge they were rational and sane and just needed therapy. They failed.

Relatives in California had taken the boys in and they'd changed their identities to keep them safe once their parents had been released from jail. That had been fifteen years ago. Luca trusted only Mike. Mike trusted only Luca.

He couldn't bear to think of his little brother being gone. Not gone. Not forever. The world needed people like Luca.

What if . . . what if their parents had found Luca?

No. It was impossible. Their parents had each spent fourteen years in prison. Their father was now wheelchair bound due to Multiple Sclerosis, and their mother had Alzheimer's. At least, that's what the police had told Mike. Both parents were in minimum security medical facilities monitored by the state of Texas.

Mike didn't care what happened to them, as long as they stayed far away from him and Luca.

We keep picking the worst people for us. Why did we have to learn to fear love? How do we give up the feeling we're just not good enough to be happy?

And just like that, the rain came back.

It always gets me down. Isn't that how the song goes?

His cell phone rang and he checked the readout, blinking a couple of times in sheer amazement.

Luca.

CHAPTER SIX

"Luca?" Mike screamed his brother's name in jubilation. Keanu's head swiveled in his direction, but then came the sickening sound of Liam's voice.

Keanu hovered, his excitement changing to a look of worry as Mike's heart sank.

"What's going on?" he asked.

"The readout says Luca, but it's Liam."

"Sorry, Mike," Liam said on the other end of the phone.

Mike put him on loudspeaker as Liam said, "I probably shouldn't have done that. I changed the name on my phone to his. I had to talk to you."

Mike was speechless. He'd never been so angry in his life. Another lyric from the Carpenters' song came to mind. *Some kind of lonely clown . . .*

Enough was enough. He'd been Liam's fool for far too long.

He took his ex-lover off the speaker phone and muttered into the phone, "It's over Liam. This is without doubt the cruelest thing you could have done to me."

Keanu moved quietly away to give him privacy, marshaling the other volunteers to search another spot.

Mike railed at Liam. "I'm out here with a bunch of total strangers who have very kindly volunteered their free time to search for Luca. Honestly. It's reaffirmed my faith in human beings. We've been here all day in blinding heat one minute, pouring rain the next. I'm getting to learn there are some really wonderful people out there. You are not one of them."

"But Mike—"

"You and I? We're done. You can try and take my cat but I'm calling Heidi to come take him. I'll make sure she has a police escort to get him away from you. He's my cat. And I love him. I'm coming back for him. But not for you. I'll take this all the way to court if I have to. Just leave me alone, Liam. You're such a jerk."

"Mike—"

But Mike didn't wait to hear what he had to say. He ended the call, shaking his head in amazement. He contacted Heidi who seemed astonished that Mike had left Herman in Liam's care.

"You should have called me. I'm heading over there now. I know couple of guys who'll come with me. And don't forget, I've got a neighbor who's a cop. Leave it with me. I'll kick Liam's ass!"

"Everything okay?" Keanu came back to Mike, looking anxious.

"My ex. Can you believe he called me, disguising his number as my brother's?"

Keanu stared at him. "I thought that's what he said, but I couldn't believe it. What kind of person does that?"

"A rotten one. I've had it with him."

"Good for you. Hey. The rain's really gonna come down hard now. We should get going."

"Okay." Mike felt out of sorts and exhausted as they all walked back to their vehicles. Everybody hugged him and wished him good luck before they drove away. He was touched when Quirinne handed him a folded piece of paper with everyone's number.

"Keanu didn't tell you this, but he's my big brother." She gave Mike a hug. "If you need help looking for Luca tomorrow, call me yeah?"

"Yeah. I will. And thank you, Quirinne."

"My pleasure. And if you want to grab a coffee or even a free hula lesson, just holler."

"Thanks again. I can't believe Keanu didn't tell me you're his sister."

"He wants to keep you to himself. He doesn't want us to be friends."

"Hey!" Keanu said.

"It's too late, I already adore you," Mike told her.

"Hey!" Keanu said again.

Mike shook his head. "You're such a goofball."

"Thanks, sis." Keanu rolled his eyes at her but gave her a hug. "You like her better than me?" he asked Mike.

"I like her in a different way."

"Oh, please." Quirinne stuck her fingers in her ears. "Not listening!"

Mike hugged her again and she sprinted to her car.

"Want to go back to Hawaii Kai or you want to hang out at my place until I go to meet Greg at five?"

"I want to hang out with you."

"Cool." Keanu looked happy.

"I really need to get my car."

"Why? Don't you like my driving?"

"Your driving is excellent, but you can't keep taking me everywhere."

"Why not?"

"You're working tomorrow, remember?"

Keanu's face fell. "You're no fun."

They got into the car and headed back into town. Halfway down the mountain the rain stopped. Mike could actually turn and see the rain behind them.

"That's so weird!" he exclaimed.

"One of the many paradoxes of the island life." Mike turned on the radio. The Carpenters were singing "Rainy Days and Mondays."

"This song has all the right ideas. We need rain so we can know the sun. We have to have loss to appreciate love. You've known a lot of loss in your life, haven't you, Mike?"

"Yeah. I guess I have."

"Me, too. Takes one to know one." Keanu reached over and squeezed his knee. Next thing Mike knew, Keanu pulled over and they leaned into each other for the most searing kiss Mike had ever experienced. He liked the way Keanu kissed him.

Keanu broke off their breathless embrace first, looking around him.

"I know I'm not on the force anymore but I don't normally sit in my car in broad daylight kissing other men."

"Good," Mike said and cupped Keanu's head with both hands, drawing the man back to him.

Their first kiss had been no idle daydream. There was serious heat between them. Mike liked everything Keanu did, the way he explored his mouth with his tongue, the soft, erotic little sighs, the nips with lips and teeth melding into deep, soul searching kisses.

"Damn," Keanu said when they broke away a second time. "I thought I'd never hit this milestone."

"Milestone?" Mike was still dizzy from the impact of Keanu's mouth roaming his.

"Yeah. I think I just met a guy who's pretty amazing."

Mike gulped. "Back at you."

They smiled at each other.

"You really want me to take you to pick up your car?"

"Maybe later," Mike said.

"I like the way you think."

Keanu suddenly took his foot of the brake and the vehicle almost collided with the one ahead of them.

"Oops," he said. "Guess it's time to go home."

Home turned out to be an apartment off a street called

Pilikoi in the non-tourist area of Waikiki. As they rose up the elevator to the seventh floor, Mike stopped to admire the ocean views from the open windows. To his left, the mountains Keanu told him were the Ko'olau Range, loomed like large jewels. To his right, sand and surf beckoned. He didn't look straight down.

"Come on." Keanu pulled him away toward his apartment. It was an interesting building, older style with only six units on each floor.

Mike liked the decor as soon as he was inside Keanu's spacious interior.

Surfboards and trophies lined one wall.

"Wages of a misspent youth," Keanu said, when Mike walked over to study the array of prizes and ribbons.

The huge sliding doors that led to the lanai looked over a grotto-style pool with tiki totems and gigantic multi-hued hibiscus bushes.

"This is lovely. A real Hawaiian paradise."

"Thanks. I think so. Say, you ever tried linguini?"

"The pasta? Sure. But I'm not really hungry."

"No, not pasta. The sexual position."

"Er, no. I haven't. I didn't even know there was such a thing."

"Well, thank God you met me then." Keanu took him by the hand and led him to his bedroom.

"Nice bed."

"I think so. It's new. Let's try it out." Keanu pushed him none too gently onto the mattress.

"Bouncy," Mike said between kisses as Keanu lay atop him exploring his mouth once more.

Is it wrong to be this turned on when my brother's missing?

Mike ignored the thought. He could worry again in a few minutes.

Oh, boy. Keanu's tongue had dipped beneath the neckline of Mike's T-shirt.

Mike was putty in Keanu's capable hands.

Soon both men were naked.

Man, oh man, Keanu had a fearsome shark surfer god's body and a nice juicy cock standing straight up.

"Lie on your side, that's right, like that," Keanu whispered in Mike's ear before putting a pillow under his head for extra support.

He knelt behind Mike's ass, leaning ever-so-slightly over his body. Mike heard him uncapping a bottle.

"Lotus oil," Keanu murmured, his warm hands sliding over Mike's shoulders and back. Long, sweeping movements turned to smaller, tighter circles as he worked Mike's tired muscles and then slid over his ass and down his thighs. The ripple effect of his fingers pressing into Mike's flesh was pleasure and pain combined.

Keanu's hands moved to Mike's belly and, mercifully, to Mike's cock, which was just aching for some attention.

Tension fell away as Keanu bent over Mike's thighs and sucked Mike's cock into his tight mouth. He reached up to press the fingers of one hand into the base of Mike's skull. With the other, he encircled Mike's balls. He released his cock and moved his hand to Mike's ass.

A finger, then, a second one began working his ass crack.

Mike held his breath as Keanu rubbed Mike's asshole, then the back of his hand ran down to Mike's perineum. Mike humped that warm hand for a moment.

He listened as Keanu tore into a foil square and gloved up.

Keanu kept rubbing, then lowered his face to lick Mike for a moment before pushing one of his knees between Mike's legs. He positioned himself to penetrate Mike. He put one hand on Mike's hip to support himself as he took the plunge.

"Relax," Keanu whispered, rocking and fucking Mike into a sea of pleasure. The late afternoon sun crossed his face as Keanu worked his way into him.

Keanu might have wanted Mike to relax but he never stopped moving himself. The friction from the positions they were in got them both into a frenzy in no time. Keanu gripped Mike's cock with one hand, his hip with the other and fucked Mike to an orgasm he wouldn't forget in a hurry before exploding inside Mike himself.

"And that my friend is why it's called linguini. I just turned us both into limp noodles." Keanu kissed the back of Mike's neck and wrapped himself around him.

"I eat pasta this way," Mike said, already drifting off to sleep. "I use my spoon and wrap the noodles around the fork and . . ."

Mike had disturbing dreams of his brother calling out to him. "Mike! Mike!" When Mike turned around, Luca was in Serenity's house, running his hand across a tabletop saying, "Teak."

He jolted awake, aware of the smell of coffee and the sound of running water.

Keanu came over to the bed. "I hate to wake you, but we should take a shower. You want to wait for me here while I go meet Greg, or you want to pick up your car?"

"I should get the car."

"Of course." Keanu looked disappointed. "I'll call you when it's over."

"I hope he's honest with you."

"I hope so, too. Wanna save water and shower with a new friend?"

Friend? Is that all we are? Mike brushed aside the letdown he was feeling.

He jumped into the shower with Mike, who lent him a brand new T-shirt before pouring coffee into travel tumblers for each of them.

"I don't want to go," Mike suddenly said.

"Come and stay tonight. I'll throw some steaks on the grill. I'll call you as soon as I know something."

Mike nodded. He liked Keanu and had enjoyed making linguini with the guy. He felt apprehensive about him going off to meet Greg.

"I've got a bad feeling about this."

"It's not a date," Keanu said changing socks for the third time.

"No, it's not that. He's a really creepy guy," Mike warned.

"I know, honey. I'm doing this for Luca. And for you."

Mike nodded. "Why do you keep changing socks?"

"Because you've got me all flustered and I can't find a pair that matches."

"I'll help you."

"No you don't. Stay over there. If you put a hand on me, I'll get us both naked again." He scowled. "I like you naked, Mike deCosta."

"I like you naked too, naked chef. You know any other human noodle dishes?"

"Plenty." Keanu wiggled his brows. "I'll show you some later."

They left the apartment, Mike checking his cell phone for messages. Six missed calls from Luca. Man, Liam needed to give up this shit.

Outside, they got in the car and Mike noticed a car parked across the road, a man behind the wheel pretending to read a newspaper.

"You've been seeing too many movies, honey," Keanu said as they drove off.

Hey, the guy was right. Mike loved movies, and paranoia had become second nature in his life.

Keanu dropped him at the Jensen lot and gave him a quick kiss. "Wish me luck."

"It's wished." Mike winked at him and got out of the

vehicle. It was strange being alone again. He found his car among the stalls and realized all his stuff was in the back of Keanu's car. All he had on him were his wallet and cell phone.

I could drive to the Melissa Hotel, where Keanu's meeting Greg. I need my laptop, right? That's a good excuse. In the meantime, I could be there. Watching. I could be part of the backup team. Just to be polite.

The more he thought about it, the more he liked the idea. He Googled the hotel and found that it was on Kalakaua Avenue. Ah, back to the maze of one-way streets. He pressed all the necessary buttons to get the voice-activated directions and he made his way out of the lot.

I'm doing great so far. I've missed the exit three times!

He circled one more time and finally shot out of the exit. As he found his way to the freeway he was aware of being followed.

Man, I think it's the guy who was parked outside Keanu's place.

Mike panicked and missed the freeway entrance. The female voice on his GPS announced, "Recalculating."

The man tailing him got awfully close. He bumped Mike's fender. Mike took off and hit the freeway, heading away from Waikiki. He drove to the Pali Highway exit and somehow wound up back on the H1 heading back to Waikiki.

He looked in the rearview mirror. The man who'd been tailing him had gone.

Phew.

He followed the patient navigator's instructions, taking his time, driving slowly. He ignored the blast of car horns and the flipped birds as irate drivers drove around him.

Geez, we're on an island! What's the rush?

He took the Queen Emma Street exit as advised. It seemed to him that the female voice had started to turn terse.

"Turn left! Recalculating."

He was beginning to hate that word almost as much as he hated the word *teak*.

Mike finally made it to another street named after a queen and then made a left onto Kalakaua Avenue.

Holy crap!

The car was back behind him!

He turned to look over his shoulder and shot right through a red light, narrowly missing a tiki trolley loaded with Japanese tourists.

The car that followed him roared off, and with a rueful wave Mike drove on toward Diamond Head. It was five after five. Hopefully Greg would be late.

He turned left at one of the last streets on Kalakaua. The Melissa was on the corner of the main drag and Paoakalani.

Mike was stunned to find metered parking right out front. He made sure to park correctly to avoid a ticket and was dismayed to discover the meter was only good for half an hour.

He emptied what felt like his entire life savings into the meter. He'd just have to come back out again. Soon. Mike raced into the hotel just in time to see Noah and Alvin frog-marching Greg away from the entrance.

"Mike! Thank God! These assholes think I've done something to Luca. Tell them. Tell them I love him! I'd never hurt him. You know that!"

The two officers stopped moving.

"You hurt him all the time," I snarled. "You treat my brother like he's a piece of garbage."

"No, I don't," he whined.

Keanu joined them out front, brandishing his cell phone.

"I've got somebody on the line here who wants to talk to you, Mike."

"Who?"

"Luca," he said. "The *real* Luca."

"What does he mean by the real Luca?" Greg griped as the officers took him away.

Mike held his breath. "Luca?" he asked, almost bursting

into tears when his brother said,

"Yeah, Mike. It's me."

"I never meant for you to worry, I just wanted to get away from Greg. I came here for a couple of days with a guy I met." Luca's words came out in a breathless rush.

"What guy? Where are you?"

"I'm on the twelfth floor of the Melissa Hotel. I made a real bad mistake, Mike. Greg said he'd found us a hot guy for a threesome, but he was a drug dealer. He handcuffed me and kept me in his room, in exchange for all the drugs Greg wanted."

It took everything in me to remain calm. "Are you okay?"

A pause. "Yeah. The police arrested Greg. Can you believe he pimped me out like that?"

Yes, I can. Aloud he said, "I'm so sorry, Luca. Are you okay?" he asked again.

"I will be. I've got a black eye and I wanna sleep for a hundred years, but, man, if you hadn't met Keanu I'd still be tied to this bed, servicing whoever Greg could get money from."

He started to cry.

"I want to see him," Mike told Keanu.

"I'll take you up there." Keanu put his arm around Luca and steered him inside. On the other end of the phone, Luca sobbed harder.

"I don't want you to see me like this."

"I'm your brother. I'm here to help."

In the elevator, Mike tried to comprehend everything that had just gone down.

"The abandoned car was staged. The landlady was in on it from the beginning, but she ratted out Greg when he stopped paying her off," Keanu told him.

"Oh, my God."

"Greg's going to do some serious time. He drugged and

beat up your brother. Hired him out on three different social networking sites. Luca's with the hotel doctor now, but he seems to be doing pretty well."

Mike had no idea what to say except, "Thank you."

"You can imagine my shock when I met Greg and he took me straight up to the room and there's your brother shackled to the bed."

Mike thought he might collapse from the stress of it all.

Keanu was right there with him as he went to see his brother.

Luca looked pretty bad, but insisted he was fine. The doctor however wanted to put him in the hospital for observation.

"His blood pressure is soaring because of the drugs and he is badly dehydrated. His heartbeat is still erratic but better than it was fifteen minutes ago. He's had a bad shock and a heavy mix of narcotics were forced into his system," the doctor said. "I would like to get him on a saline drip and monitor him. I am a little worried he may experience tremors as we clean out his system."

Mike agreed, and he and Keanu drove Luca to Queen's Hospital where the staff all knew Keanu.

One of the nurses said, "You get shot again, Keanu?"

"Not today, Auntie," he responded.

Mike was grateful that his brother was in such good hands.

"He needs rest and a lot of hydration," the nurse said. "You come back later tonight and visit him. Bring him soup. Soup is good."

Aye, aye, Captain!

Keanu steered Mike out of the door again.

"I should get my car," Mike said.

"Yeah, I guess you should. Wanna come home with me?"

"I think I do. But when Luca is ready to get out, I should take him to a hotel and not Serenity's place."

"I guess." Keanu didn't look very happy about it. "Let's

talk about it later. I think we can work something out."

"Yeah?"

"Yeah. I know about these things. I have a sixth sense you know."

"You've mentioned that before."

Mike felt better. He was relieved his brother was alive and okay. Even if Mike did have a parking ticket. Oh, well. A small price to pay.

"Follow me home, beautiful. I want to show you another favorite recipe of mine."

"Yeah, which one?"

"You'll see."

Mike couldn't wait.

"And Mike?"

"Uh-huh."

"I think your cat will love Hawaii. We just might need a bigger place and I guess I'd better start giving Luca judo lessons."

Mike looked at him. "But you just met me."

"No. I met you yesterday. And if there's one thing I've learned, it's from the Carpenters. The line that always sticks in my mind is *the only thing to do is run and find the one who loves me.*"

Mike looked at him. "Yeah. Rainy days and Mondays used to get me down. Not anymore."

A big fat raindrop fell from the sky.

"Get in the car and follow me, Mike. I want to be alone with you."

Mike gulped and did as he was told. He was three blocks from Keanu's apartment when a new Rumi quote for the day hit his inbox.

If I bring you to mind, you're there in my thoughts.
If I open my mouth, you're there on my lips.
If I'm happy, you're the secret to it.

– Rumi

Yep, the Carpenters, Rumi, and Keanu sure knew a lot about love. And life. For the first time ever, Mike thought he could love and feel safe. And that somehow, some way, Luca would feel those things, too.

I'll show him how to run and find the one who loves him.

The one who is the secret to his happiness.

The one who can help make rainy days and Mondays the best days to smile.

YOU MAY ALSO ENJOY THE FOLLOWING FROM EXTASY BOOKS INC:

The Book and The Rose
A.J. Llewellyn

Excerpt

"So . . . Evans . . . is it okay if I call you Evans?"

It's my name, dumbass. "Sure."

"I know you had a really great run and some hot numbers with Out of Step." He took a deep breath.

Oh, here we go.

"So tell me, how is Nora doing? Is it true she's in a lock-down facility?"

In the four weeks since he'd been actively hunting for a new job, Evans had been able to sift interviewers into two categories. Those genuinely interested in maybe giving him work, and those who wanted fresh Nora North gossip.

"She's in rehab and doing great, but as I am sure you're aware, her health comes first, and the network decided to pull the plug on the show. After all, she is . . . was the show."

Mitch swung in his chair. "Right, right. So tell me, is there any truth to the rumor that she took off her clothes and went running through the Paramount lot begging strange guys to fuck her?"

Shit! How much does he know? She even begged me and I'm gay!

"No. Absolutely not."

Mitch kept asking questions. Evans moved Mitch into Category B, bit down on his disappointment and bantered, feigning interest, allowing his mind to wander. He could drift and dream . . . alone on his own mental private island with Mio-Alejo Cortez, the hot Spanish businessman he'd had not just one, but two scorching encounters with. Just the thought of that man's sensuous mouth on his body made him squirm in his seat.

God, I want to call him, but I have to play it cool.

Evans still couldn't believe his luck meeting Mio on that brief trip to London. He'd never seen a man who oozed so much sex appeal. His dark, silky hair had been cropped short, but still managed to look dreamy with his widow's peak and thick, dark brows. He didn't smile much, but when he did, he was electrifying. His English had been limited when they met in the bar at the Dorchester. The second time he'd run into Mio, the man had whipped out a Spanish-English dictionary.

He'd smooth out a piece of paper on which he'd written, I crave to speak to you. That paper was still in his wallet. It carried Evans through some tough times dealing with his bleak moments in the Hollywood minefield.

"You are more than handsome," Mio had said. "You are beautiful."

They'd spent the afternoon and evening in bed. Lips, eyes, mouth, tongue, teeth . . . there wasn't a part of him I didn't like . . . or spend hours lingering over.

A late supper and a night of unhurried, but passionate, nonstop sex had ruined Evans for any of the studio idiots he met back in Los Angeles.

"You know, I met her once at a party up on Summit," Mitch was saying when Evans tuned back to the present.

Evans knew where this conversation was heading and didn't want to take this road at all. Just saying Summit was an industry catchword. It meant that Mitch partied — hard — and wanted to know if Evans did. Or if Evans knew about those big pool-and-sex parties up on luxurious but decadent Summit Drive.

"I know nothing about her . . . partying," Evans said. "Look, she's a friend. A friend I care deeply about. I wish her the best. I'm sure you do, too."

She fucking killed my career and my show. A show that took me six years to get into production. Right now, I fucking hate her.

"Right, right. You're right." Mitch pointed a finger at him. "She was hittin' the snort pretty hard though and . . ."

He allowed Mitch to ramble on. Evans wanted to think about Mio. Mio, who'd called him from Spain three weeks ago saying he had a business trip to Miami.

"Meet me," he'd implored. "My hands . . . they need to touch you. My mind . . . it needs you. You are my tesoro."

His treasure? Evans would have flown anywhere, on his own dime to see him, but having another man value him enough to fly him out first-class for a hot weekend had been alluring. They'd met at the airport . . . oh, what pleasure it had been to see Mio in his trademark Saville Row suit and hand-sewn Turnbull and Asser shirt.

Their chemistry had been undeniable . . . even more intense. They both knew their first fling had been no fluke.

He hadn't bothered Mio with much of the drama of getting Nora into lockdown, the surgery she required after destroying her septum, the cartilage between her nostrils, due to snorting so much coke. Losing the show. He'd been so delighted with the respite, the adoring attention of his handsome, debonair lover. He smiled, thinking of Mio's childlike glee in buying Chicken McNuggets, dipping them in honey and feeding them in bed to Evans . . .

Now he'd been back two weeks and two days. Each day without Mio got worse. They talked at least once a day and the calls became shorter and shorter. It hurt them both to talk . . . and also, not to talk. Evans felt tears pricking the back of his eyes. Mio had been a beautiful dream that both harmed and helped him. In some moments, he could imagine a future with him. In other moments, the slender, invisible thread between them seemed to snap.

"So what are you working on now?" Mitch asked.

Evans jerked back to reality. "I've been wanting to meet with you about doing a new series with Heliconia."

"Right, right . . ."

It galled that Out of Step had been his entire creation and now it was locked in contract hell with the network. He couldn't use the name or recast the lead. He had to start again.

"The thing of it is that we're not looking to get involved in television right now."

Evans remembered that last afternoon with Mio. They'd gone for a swim at the hotel pool. Mio had run into a couple of guys he knew and introduced them to Evans. They'd been such good-looking men, but before the conversation could start, Mio whisked Evans back to their room.

He was amazing. Tender . . . passionate . . . funny. I'll never meet anyone like him ever again. But our lives are separate. Ha. You might even say out of step. I need to be here, and he's as European as olive oil.

Evans smiled at Mitch. "You approached me about your new vampire series. We were supposed to—"

"Vampires are passé now, Evans. Fantastic name by the way. It's your mom's last name, right?"

"Yes."

Why did you bring me here if vampires are on the slide?

He contemplated asking the question out loud. He had nothing to lose except his health benefits, but Mitch answered it for him.

"Zombies are where it's at. Zombies are the new vampires."

"Absolutely," Evans said. "Which is what I wanted to talk to you about."

I can switch my pitch to zombies . . . but I thought they were hot two years ago.

"We already have two zombie shows slated. Two movies . . . if they fly, I'd like to talk to you about running a series for us."

Fuck! That could take another year . . .

"In the meantime, I was wondering . . . I don't have a job I can give you, but I thought . . . you know . . . maybe we could have dinner one night . . . soon?"

Mio's body . . . hard, smooth, skin the color of caramel . . . yet he couldn't keep his mouth off mine.

"No," he said. "I'm involved."

"Oh . . ." That threw Mitch. He was used to being the guy in charge, clearly. "That's weird . . . only I asked around, and word on the vine is that you're single."

"I don't . . ." Evans took a breath. "I'm pretty private, Mitch." He stood. "Thanks for the meeting. I really appreciate your time."

Mitch scrambled out of his chair. "Oh . . . well, thank you. Uh . . . have a nice day."

Evans shook his hand and looked him in the eye. "You have a nice day, too, Mitch." You jerk.

He walked out of the office, past Silvia's desk. She didn't glance up at him, and he knew she'd listened to the whole thing. She didn't look up because the business meeting had gone badly and her boss's clumsy attempt at getting a date had flopped.

This was the latest in technological progress. Studio executives bugged their offices during meetings so that pesky writers couldn't claim they'd stolen ideas after pitch meetings, which they routinely did.

"Thank you, Silvia," he said, mindful of being polite and friendly with her. Today's personal assistant could be tomorrow's studio boss.

She glanced up, smiled and also wished him a nice day.

Yeah, nice. He stood outside and checked his cell phone for

messages. He longed for a call, just one little text from Mio. He remembered their last moments, Mio between his legs, fucking him, his mouth clamped over Evans'.

I never wanted to leave him.

He called his agent, Kelly King, who took his call immediately.

"How did it go?"

"A bust. He wanted a date."

"I hope you said yes."

He laughed.

"Are you going over to visit Nora?" she asked.

"Yeah."

"Well, you'll need a drink after that. It's on me. I'll meet you over at Residuals. Let's say one?"

"Are you kidding me? I don't start that early."

"Oh, excuse me." He loved Kelly. She always made him laugh. "How's five o'clock?"

"Sounds good to me."

He ended the call, got into his six-month-old Prius and thought about calling his assistant, Michael, who was hanging by a thread emotionally and financially. Evans helped the guy out with bills and with constant pep talks. When the show was canceled, he'd promised Michael he'd find them a job, he'd take him with him. Nora North's drug addiction had not just wrecked his show, she'd demolished the hopes of the wonderful crew Evans had fought hard to assemble.

Now it looked like she had ruined his career. He was being punished for her sins in Hollywood.

I'm all washed up, and I'm only thirty-two.

Evans pushed out of the parking lot and hit a red light. It was a long one. He sat, not wanting to listen to music or talk radio. All he wanted was Mio's smile. To hear his laugh one more time. The sun sparkled, and it should have heartened him after long weeks of unprecedented rain. Except that high above him overlooking Riverside Drive, the poster of perky, pretty Nora North promoting Out of Step, a poster that had been there for months was being covered up.

He watched the workmen with long-handled sticks pasting up the long, single sheets that would make one gigantic poster.

A part of him wanted to step on the gas and go straight out into the intersection and let the other, unsuspecting drivers kill him. A part of him wanted to . . . no, needed to stay alive in case Mio called.

His cell phone rang, and he plugged it into his dashboard circuit.

"Hello," he said.

"Hola, Evans."

The light turned green, and a car honked him from behind.

It was him. It was Mio.

ABOUT THE AUTHOR

A.J. Llewellyn lives in California, but dreams of living in Hawaii. Frequent trips to all the islands, bags of Kona coffee in her fridge and a healthy collection of Hawaiian records keep this writer refueled. A.J. loves male/male erotica, has a passion for all animals — especially the dog, the cat and the turtle. A.J. believes that love is a song best sung out loud.

To find out more about A. J., visit her website at www.ajllewellyn.com or you can email her at AJ@AJLlewellyn.com.

www.ingramcontent.com/pod-product-compliance
Lightning Source LLC
Chambersburg PA
CBHW070224140626
46555CB00018B/1266